STIGMATA

STIGMATA

A novel by
Symone Dashell

Printed in the United States of America
First Printing, 2020

ISBN 978-1-7359807-1-3

Cover art: Loui Jover

Publisher: Brittney Holmes Jackson & Co.
Stonecrest, GA 30038
www.BrittneyHolmesJackson.com

Dedication

This novel is dedicated to the fulfillment of the God-ordained purpose set out before me. It is also dedicated to those individuals who read it and those lives that it changes. I dedicate this to you.

Acknowledgments

Thank you, God, for revealing my purpose and allowing it to come into fruition.

Thank you to my family, friends, and loved ones that have walked with me through this whole creation process. You know exactly who you are. Without the support, prayers, and listening ears, I would not
have been able to push through the tough times.

Thank you to my social media friends and family for all of the support and encouragement.

"All that we see or seem is but a dream within a dream."
- Edgar Allan Poe

Part 1:

The

Wilderness

Chapter 1

Present Day

"Please! Stop! I did not try to kill myself! It was her!" I yelled and struggled against the restraints as the first responders strapped me to the stretcher.

They paused and asked, "Who are you speaking about, ma'am?" I glanced over at my fiancé, Aaron, who was in tears. I looked back at the men and slumped back in defeat. I knew that they would not believe me if I told them that there was another person that did this. They rolled me into the ambulance and took me directly to Goshen Psychiatric Hospital. On the way there, I thought about the fact that I was a mess and had known this for a long time. I was surprised that Aaron hadn't contacted the proper authorities much earlier.

6 Years Earlier

Noelle and I were inseparable. We were both from Winchester, Virginia and we met when we were just kids in elementary school. We lived in the same neighborhood as children rode to school together after our parents found out that we went to the same school. We grew up together through middle school and high school. We even had our first jobs together at a fast food restaurant. We had birthday parties, heartbreaks, and breakthroughs together. We had even been told we looked alike. We both had brown hair, brown eyes, mocha-colored skin, were 5'2 in height, and wore the same size in clothes and shoes.

We also attended the same church where we realized a similar desire to continue our future in ministry.

When we made it past our grade school years, we decided to attend the same college, a theological seminary school in Pennsylvania. I chose the track of Christian Counseling while she chose to get her degree in Biblical Archaeology. We had plans to combine our degrees and create a business and podcast series.

A frequent topic of discussion between us was how great things were going in our lives, how we had the best friendship, how blessed we were, and how we completely trusted God to do things abundantly and exceedingly more than what we could have ever expected. We acknowledged these things, but we also talked about what we would do if something happened to either one of us, our unwavering faith, and healing. We always tried to stay prepared because we knew that life would happen. Unfortunately, we had built our lives while sporting rose-colored glasses.

...

The phone rang three times as I waited for Noelle to answer. It was our break between classes, and I knew that this would be my only opportunity to speak with her before our movie night tonight.

"Hey, Mya!" She sounded so excited to hear from me.

"Hey, Noelle!" I said just as enthusiastically and laughed.

"So, I just wanted to check in with you because our movie night is tonight. Right?" I asked. I could hear her rummaging through some papers.

"Uh, yeah! We have so much to catch up on. It's been so hectic lately."

"Okay. What do you want to eat?"

"Chips, salsa, and tacos from our favorite food truck." I could have guessed that one. I started to reply as she began to speak to someone else. She turned her focus back to her phone, let me know that she would see me later and that she was excited, and hung up.

After the call, I proceeded through the rest of my day. My last class was a Bible study course where we did an in-depth study of the Old Testament. This was one of the core classes for this particular school and we were currently in the book of Numbers.

As soon as the class ended, I went to pick up the chips, salsa, and tacos and went home to prepare the movie. When we moved to Pennsylvania for college, we chose to rent a house. We had been saving our money from our jobs and preparing for this. We thought that the house was a great idea at first, but as time progressed, we started calling our landlord more and more. Pipes were leaking, there was what appeared to be mildew in the corner of Noelle's bedroom towards the front of the house, there was

3

a cracked window in my room which was near the back of the house, and the plumbing system was not the best.

When I finally made it home, there was a peculiar smell. It had a tinge of gas or something burning so I briefly looked around in the kitchen, but I didn't see a source for the scent, so I assumed that it was something outside. I eventually forgot about it as I continued to prepare for movie night.

Noelle made it home around 8:30 pm. She took a shower and then jumped on the couch next to me where we immediately started to eat and watch the comedy we had chosen. After the movie, we talked, laughed, and caught up until we both fell asleep on the couch. Around 1:30 am, I woke up and went to bed and left Noelle sleeping peacefully on the couch.

I was startled awake around 4:00 in the morning by the sound of screaming. The smell from earlier was extremely pungent and I was overheated. I got up to see where the screams were coming from, but as I got closer to my door, I saw an orange flickering underneath. I started to panic and screamed Noelle's name, but all I could hear was her high-pitched screaming. I found my phone and made my way to my window. Smoke was beginning to seep into my room, so I had to escape. The window would not budge so I used my phone to break it and glass shattered everywhere. I climbed through, landed on the ground in a confused heap, dialed 911, and ran to the front of the house. As I was running, the operator answered the phone, and I began yelling out my address. I froze when I realized that the entire front of the house was engulfed in bright orange and red flames and black smoke. There I was, small and helpless, standing in blue shorts and a pink shirt, unable to move, unable to think. After a few seconds, I realized that I could no longer hear Noelle's screams which had to have meant that she made it out of the house and was running around looking for me, so I took another lap around the house. After my lap, when I realized that Noelle was not outside, my mind started to go in circles. There was no way for me to run to the front door because of the angry flames. All I could do was wait along with the other people that had started to emerge from their homes. Wait and cry.

I heard the wails from the sirens and ran towards the street while waving my arms. My tears blinded me as I started screaming inaudible words, trying to tell them that my friend was still in the house. In a frenzy, they prepared the hose and began spraying, which calmed the flames. After about two minutes, there was only smoke. They carefully ran into what I once called my home while I was questioned and prodded by one of the first responders. His voice sounded muffled as if I had cotton in my ears. He looked like a hazy cartoon character. I couldn't make sense of any of this.

I got excited as I heard a deep voice yell, "We found someone!" A couple of seconds later, a man walked up to me with a haunted expression. I fell to the ground because I knew that they had not found "someone." They had found a body -her body. Darkness surrounded me.

I woke up in the hospital. I had a few bandages, but nothing serious. In the movies, after a traumatic situation, people wake up in the hospital and ask, "what happened?" No. Not me. I knew exactly what had happened. I remembered every single, painful moment. I looked up and saw my parents, flowers, cards, and balloons. My parents rushed to me when they saw that I was awake and held me as the tears began to fall. I was shaking and inconsolable until the calming medicine finally put me back to sleep. I thank God that He gave me dreams of happiness because my reality was the complete opposite. It was comparable to the contrast between Heaven and Hell.

The funeral was, well, a funeral. My parents and I sat with Noelle's family. We were her family. The whole time I was seated in that movie-theater style chair in that modern church, I asked God "why" in my head. By the time we made it to the burial site, I had asked why so many times that my mind was tired and delusional.

After my best friend was six feet beneath the ground, I still wanted to talk to her about all of this. My mind told me that I was going to go home, call her, and talk this hurt through. My rational thinking left and buried itself in the freshly turned ground with Noelle.

As I turned to walk away from where she was buried, I noticed that things looked completely different from the area surrounding me. There were many people in the far distance for as far as I could see. They were grimy looking and appeared to be exhausted. They were working in what looked to be a desert that seemed to be extremely hot, and, somehow, I felt like I knew them even though I had never seen them. The whole scene looked as if it came out of a movie or book about ancient times. I looked down at my feet and the green grass that surrounded me and, when I looked back up, the vision was gone. The distance now matched where I was currently standing—no working people. No desert.

When I got home, I rushed to the bathroom and splashed my face with cold water because I felt hot. When I looked in the mirror, I saw a different person looking back at me. She resembled the people I had seen working in the desert when I was at the burial site. Somehow, I knew her even though I had never seen her before this moment. I also knew that her name was Meira. I was scared, so I looked away quickly, putting my face in my hands. I said a quick prayer, and when I looked back up, I saw my face, the face of Mya Afad, looking back at me.

Remember those rose-colored glasses that I previously mentioned? That day, those glasses fell to the ground and shattered revealing a much darker reality...or two.

Chapter 2

Present day

I was sitting slumped over slightly in the chair across from Dr. Silvia Horia who talked way too much for my liking. I thought that I was supposed to be the one talking. Two weeks ago, my fiancé, Aaron, decided to call the psychiatric hospital because he believed that I was "suicidal." Meira, the Israelite girl who existed within me, was simply trying to escape the misery of being stuck in the wilderness. She and the Israelites were there for so long that I came to understand her, but I just knew that no one else would.

I looked at Dr. Horia. She had thin, brownish hair, average brown eyes, light-brown skin, a small, straight frame, and an annoying mouth covered with bright red lipstick that I wished she would remove from her front tooth, but I refused to speak up. She went on about how I needed to open up to be released and how she knew I wanted to get back to my family. How did she know? I believed that it might have been safer for me in the hospital. Out there, in the real world, my two lives were becoming exhausting to maintain. I ate, slept, and didn't even think twice about my worldly responsibilities in Goshen Psychiatric Hospital.

"Mya, please take some time to do the work that I am providing you to complete outside of our sessions." She instructed me in a calm voice.

I never did the assignments and didn't care enough to do them. "I hear you." I responded. I'm sure she was used to dealing with people that were not very receptive. I had to give it to her, she was definitely consistent, but I was just happy that our 30-minute session was over.

"Mya, please understand that we are here for you and that we support your growth process. What would help you open up at this moment.

"Honestly, I am not sure. I can't bring myself to think about those things right now."

"I understand. This can be a lot to take in. Please know that your reaction is normal, and we will continue to be here until you are ready."

"Thank you." I smiled slightly and then got up to leave. I walked out without even saying good-bye or glancing back. I was not the best person.

There were two dayrooms in the hospital. I headed to the smaller one where there were fewer people to watch television without someone trying to talk to me or ask me to play a game. I was so annoyed by people attempting to talk to me and having to tell them "no" constantly."

I mindlessly watched television for a couple of hours until it was time for me to attempt to eat dinner and then head to bed. This was my routine, and I was fine with it for the time being.

5 ½ Years Earlier

I came back to school about 6 months ago and decided to complete a double major- Christian Counseling for me and Biblical Archaeology for Noelle. School always came easily to me, so I had no problems with keeping my grades up despite my evolving issue.

I hadn't told a single soul about it, but since the day we buried Noelle, I had been living in two different worlds. It's hard to explain. I was still functioning in regular society as Mya, but I was also Meira who lived amongst the Israelites in Egypt and in the wilderness. I was a slave, and I was a college student. Sometimes, though, my two worlds would get crossed.

Today, I was focused on passing my midterms and going back home to visit my parents for a couple of days. A little while after Noelle died, I moved into a new apartment and bought a puppy and named her Grace. We were going to be traveling home together so I could indulge in this much needed mental break.

I was sitting in class, waiting for the instructor to finish speaking and pass out the tests so I could complete it and leave when I suddenly felt hot. I knew what this temperature change signified; Meira was trying to emerge. The problem was that she saw a different world - an ancient world. She was on a completely different mission than I, which was to survive while in captivity. In contrast, my mission was to graduate from college and get a good paying job. We were in two totally different eras. I was

A.D. and she was B.C. I was here and now, and she was there and then. Do you understand my dilemma?

Luckily, I was able to complete my test quickly and leave the classroom before Meira made a mockery of me. I went home to grab my packed bags, my dog, and I left. On the road, I listened to a mixture of gospel, R&B, rap music, and podcasts, which made the drive go by quickly. Four hours later, I made it home where I was greeted by my loving mother and father, my favorite aunt Camilla, and the family cat, Frenzie, who ran right up to Grace. We hugged and spoke briefly about our plans for this visit. I took my things and Grace out of my car, went up to my old room, and sat on the bed. Every time I sat in this room, I would think about Noelle and all of the time that we spent here. It was still just as hard to think about her now as it was when she first died. When would my relief of this pain make an appearance?

I went back downstairs to my family who were talking and playing with the pets. My mom asked, "What would you like for dinner? Where would you like to go?" "I don't care where we go, as long as we go soon because I am starving," I responded. My parents and aunt laughed and started discussing a new restaurant that everyone was raving about. We dispersed to get ready and within an hour, we were heading out the door.

We were seated after a 20-minute wait when we got to the restaurant and were met at the table by our waitress. She asked us what drinks we would like and, soon after, brought them to the table. We ordered our meals and without realizing what was coming out of my mouth, I said, "Do you all serve manna ... I ... I mean, rolls? Do you all serve rolls?" I couldn't believe that Meira requested that right now. I was slightly embarrassed because even though I knew that manna was a source of sustenance for Meira and the Israelites, my family had no clue where this came from. I knew that my mother knew what manna was due to her knowledge about the Bible. She also knew full well that we didn't eat that in this day and age. The waitress and my family looked confused and slightly amused.

"Ye... yes... we do serve rolls. Let me go and grab some for you all." She hurriedly walked away, and my family took a second before continuing on with our conversation.

About an hour and a half later, we were done eating, having gotten caught up on each other's lives, and were on our way back home. When we made it to the house, I told everyone that I was going to get some rest because it had been such a long day. I went up to my room to take a shower and got in bed. For a little while, I thought about what or who was living within me, the person that was slowly but surely emerging, and how long I would be able to keep this to myself. Eventually, I drifted off into a peaceful slumber.

The next day, my aunt Camilla came over, specifically to spend time with me. She loudly entered my room at 9:00 am on the dot which jolted me awake and made Grace go into a yapping fit of anger. She

12

unnecessarily yelled, "Good morning, we're going for a walk! I'll wait for you downstairs. Be ready to go in 30 minutes." She pranced out of the room, shutting the door behind her a little too hard. "Well, looks like we're going for a walk, Gracie," I said as I rolled out of bed.

Thirty-five minutes later, Aunt Camilla, Grace, and I were walking out the front door. Even though we could have driven to a nearby park, we chose to walk around the neighborhood.

The first half of the walk was for Grace to find a spot to do her business. This process always took a long time because she would go back and forth before choosing a specific spot. After Grace finished, Aunt Camilla asked, "So, how are you? How is school?"

I took a deep breath and then responded with, "School is school. I am honestly only finishing because I know that's what Noelle would have wanted me to do for both of us. I am as good as I can be, and I trust God in this healing process because I know I can't do it on my own. How have you been?" I couldn't have been "churchier" with that generic answer.

Aunt Camilla had quite the adventure in life as well. Around the same time that Noelle passed away, her husband died from a drug overdose. Drug addiction was a battle of his since I was in elementary school. My uncle's feelings of inadequacy caused his drug issue. He was not able to produce children and even though my aunt was content with this, he couldn't come to terms with it. Regardless of the many obstacles in her marriage and with

13

her life partner, I'd always known my Aunt Camilla to have the greatest spirit and most faith through it all.

"I have my days, but I've been okay. The pain never really goes away, but you simply learn to live with it. Your uncle was suffering, so I am glad that he no longer has to deal with that," she responded and then got quiet. She was always so full of wisdom. Then she said, "I remember the last time we talked, you said that you were planning to see the counselor on your campus. Did you ever go?"

I knew this question would come up. I replied, "No, I feel like I am healing on my own. I have been praying and reading my Bible. I believe that this is what I need to get me through."

"What about church?"

"No. I haven't been going to church." I guess my tone let her know that I was not willing to elaborate.

"Well, I'm glad that you're doing something to get back to what one would consider normal. I am actually seeing a psychiatrist out here. She is really good. I learned that even though God is my source, He provides me with the necessary resources and tools to get through certain hard situations." She shared quietly.

Internally I laughed because I knew what she was doing. She had a way of getting me to understand things by using herself as an example. "I will continue to consider it," I responded even though I knew I probably wouldn't go through with it. We then talked about her sessions with her therapist and her healing process. I asked her questions because I knew what I had been experiencing and I wanted to know if this counseling stuff could really help me. I appreciated her transparency.

As we continued to walk, we got closer and closer to what appeared to be a man crouching down with another man standing over him. When we got near the men, I glanced over at them because it looked like the crouching man was making something with his hands and I wanted to see what it was. We got even closer and I could see that he was making a brick. I thought to myself, "Why is he making a brick when he can just go and buy 100 of them already made?" He also looked young but worn down and fatigued. Then I looked up at the man standing over him. He was holding a whip and he looked extremely irritated and mean. It was such a bizarre scene and I immediately thought about how the Israelites were forced to make bricks when they were under the reign of Pharaoh and before they escaped from Egypt with Moses. As a matter of fact, I was pretty sure that was exactly what I was seeing. When we got a little ahead of the two men, I glanced at Aunt Camilla, who seemed oblivious to the whole thing. Before I panicked, I asked her while motioning my head towards the two men, "Doesn't that seem weird?"

She looked at me oddly, giggled, and said, "Looks like a dad watching his son play with a toy boat in a puddle of water to me. Yeah, real weird." Definitely sarcastic. I turned my head back quickly and, of course, it was the very scene that she described. She then said, "You okay?" I replied with a nod of my head and told her that I thought we should probably head back to the house because Grace was getting tired.

We finally made it back to the house and my parents had prepared a big breakfast. I was starving so I quickly washed my hands, fixed my plate of turkey sausage, cheese grits, a biscuit, and a small amount of eggs. When we were all seated at the table, my mother said a prayer to bless the food, and we started eating. My dad asked us how the walk went, and I told him that it was great, and Aunt Camilla agreed.

"Mom, this food is so good!" I said as I chewed up my last piece of sausage.

"I'm glad you think so." She replied. We all finished the rest of our plates while talking about those "stupid reality shows" as my mother calls them.

The rest of my visit was pretty relaxing. We watched movies, played games, and laughed at YouTube videos. This was a retreat for me and I was dreading having to go back to school and face reality, but I vowed to myself that I would be in contact with my family more than ever and I even considered telling them about Meira, but I thought better of it for the time being.

Sadly, the day finally came when I had to make my way back to school. I packed all of my belongings, put Grace in the car, hugged my family goodbye, and started my drive. Just like on the way there, I listened to my music and podcasts to make the time go by fast. The only difference was that it was raining extremely hard causing me to drive a little slower.

The rain was getting abnormally hard as I drove along and started to sound like hail. When I actually paid attention to what was falling from the dark, gray-blue sky, I noticed huge bugs. Maybe ... locusts? I felt myself begin to panic and I aggressively pulled over to the side of the road because I could tell that what I was seeing was not real. When I threw the car in park, a few more of the locusts fell from the sky and then a peaceful drizzle took over that seemed to bring my temperature and heart rate back down. I took a few deep breaths, hugged Grace who was whimpering next to me, pulled back onto the road, and drove at a consistent high speed until I made it safely back to my home.

Chapter 3

Present day

It was Sunday and my parents decided to come and visit me. Just a month ago, I would have been going through one of Meira's bizarre Sabbath Sundays. Even though we couldn't do those rituals at this point, the urge still persisted.

I found them seated at a table near the back of the family room. I gave them a hug and we all sat down to talk.

"How have you been?" My mother asked.

"I've been okay. I would be even better if I weren't here." I was salty about this whole ordeal.

"Your Aunt Camilla asked about you. Would you be okay with her visiting you here sometimes?" Mom asked.

"I don't care. Whatever makes you all happy." I replied.

"Hmm ... Well, Grace is doing well. She and Frenzie are getting along and have become best friends." Mom shared enthusiastically.

"That's great." I said dryly.

"Aaron called. He says that you aren't accepting his phone calls, Mya." Mom said sadly.

"And why would I do that?" I asked sarcastically.

"Because he loves you, you love him, and you know that he was trying to help you." Mom responded, looking at me reproachfully.

"I am just not convinced that what he did was actually considered love. I really don't want to talk about him. Dad, why are you looking at me like that?" I asked my father, who was gazing at me with a sadness in his eyes.

"Well... I'm just a little sad seeing you like this. You aren't yourself and I want to see you get better soon. Have you been talking to the psychiatrist?" He asked quietly.

"I don't really have a choice, Dad. I don't believe that my issues are as bad as the other people here. I could have just done outpatient." I said as I shrugged dejectedly.

"Well, your aunt told us that she suggested that you should see a counselor previously, so you had the opportunity to do outpatient." He said with a small smile.

I wanted to roll my eyes so bad, but I knew that would be considered disrespectful. I didn't have a response because I knew it was the truth. I knew I should have seen a counselor before things escalated to this point. Accountability began to kick in and, at that moment, there was a little flicker of realization in my mind. I knew that this was the time for me to finally open up just a little. I had been in this hospital too long already and I needed to start somewhere so that I would be released.

After my parents left, I went back to my room and thought about the information that I was willing to share with the psychiatrist.

That next day, I met with Dr. Horia again. After her regular spiel, she told me that she wanted to have a conversation with me and that would require me to be as honest and transparent as possible. She tried to have this conversation previously, but I would not talk to her - I wouldn't even look at her. The first question she asked was about my personal mental health history. I told her that I had never had mental health issues before and that I didn't think my family did either. I could tell that she was delighted that I was talking. She has very strong non-verbal communication.

Next, she asked me about any traumatic experiences that I may have had prior to coming to this place. I told her the short version of what happened to Noelle.

She said, "I am sorry about your best friend." The next question she asked and was a little odd to me. "Do you ever feel as if you are under attack by your thoughts or emotions?" She questioned.

It was an interesting question because I never thought of Meira as attacking me; I just found ways to cope with her being around as much as I could. I thought for a minute and then replied, "I am not sure if I am under attack by my thoughts or emotions."

She said, "Okay, we will revisit that question when you have more clarity."

She asked me a few more questions and then said, "Now, I'd like to talk about who the "she" was that you were referring to when the ambulance arrived to take you to the hospital." This question was timed perfectly because I had spent most of the night anxious to share some of this with her.

"The 'she' that you are referring to is Meira," I said dryly. I couldn't understand why I was upset at the way that Dr. Horia spoke of her. I believed that it was because Meira had gotten offended and I could feel it.

"Okay. Can you tell me more about Meira? When did you two first meet?" Dr. Horia questioned.

"We met the day of Noelle's funeral. I looked in the mirror and saw her looking back at me. I only saw her for a few seconds."

"So, are you telling me that she is within you?" She looked inquisitively as she asked this question.

"Yes." I answered bluntly.

"What is Meira like?"

"Well ... She's not from here. I came to know her when she and the Israelites were about to leave Egypt and, when I was admitted to this place, they were all in the wilderness. She's young, but she's tired." I answered as best as I could.

Dr Horia was doing a good job of maintaining a poker face and holding in her laughter. I believed that anyone who heard this story would just laugh at me which is why I had kept it to myself.
"Why do you think she is here?"

"I don't know. The only reason that I can pinpoint the era she's is from is because of some things that she does, the visuals, and because, in class, I was reading through the Old Testament of the Bible right before all of this stuff happened."

"Does she ever try to take over?"

"Yes."

"Describe what that's like."

"Hmm … when she takes over, my temperature usually changes drastically, and I begin to see specific things as she sees them; very old and dusty. I see the people around her who also look tired. The things that she does are considered irrational by today's standards."

"Give me an example."

"Umm … at a restaurant, I accidentally called bread 'manna,' which is mostly what they ate when they were in the wilderness. There was also a time when I saw locusts falling from the sky. I even went through with a purification ritual at one point because she considered me "ceremonially unclean." Usually, when I take a moment, close my eyes, and breathe, these visions turn back into what they actually are. The locusts were just rain. I ended up here, though, because I was no longer able to blink and clear away her perspective. She became stronger and I was living in both places at the same time at all times."

"Okay. Do you ever talk to her?"

"Not verbally. It's more like thoughts. I know what she's trying to do through the thoughts that we share."

"Have you ever experienced a blackout or lost time and you can't remember what happened?"

I thought about it and one specific Sunday came to mind. "I have. One Sunday, I couldn't really control my actions and it was like I went away. When I came back or woke up a few hours later, I was wearing an ugly dress from the past, and I was sweating badly."

22

"Have you tried to remember?"

"Yes."

"What were you doing before this happened?"

"Meira and I were walking around, praying, and speaking in tongues."

"Has this happened any other time?"

"Yes, it has. There were different circumstances and some of them were more extreme than others."

"Would you like to talk about those instances?"

"Could we possibly save those for another time? I'm not ready."

"Sure. Can you tell me what happened the night that you were admitted?"

She went too far, and I shut down. I just sat quietly because I couldn't form the swarm of thoughts into words to come out of my mouth.

After a moment of silence, she said, "Is there anything else that you would like to share with me?"

"I don't think so; I just want to know why this is happening to me."

"I will begin to provide you with those answers in our next counseling session. Thank you so much for opening up to me, Mya. This is progress."

At that point, through these obscure glasses, I could now see a small glimmer of hope with a little bit of breakthrough trailing behind.

5 Years Earlier

"Okay, everyone! I want you all to find a partner; try to choose someone that you think will be reliable. This person will be your accountability partner or trust buddy for the duration of this course." Mrs. Lamire announced. "This assignment is a tradition in this Rapport Building and Assessment course because we have to understand how to effectively build relationships and trust in our personal lives to build these factors when it comes to our future clients."

It was close to the end of class and I just wanted to go home. I had this instructor last semester, and I was dreading having her again and especially on Mondays, Wednesdays, and Fridays. She wanted me to interact way more than my comfort levels allowed. I had also made a choice to not make friends which always made collaboration a problematic process.

There was a lot of shuffling and noise, but I just sat stubbornly in my chair and began to pack my things because I was ready to leave as soon as I could. About a minute later, a young man, brown-skinned, tall, and very handsome, walked up to me and politely told me that he would be keeping me accountable this semester. It was either his authority or appearance that stopped me because I had a mind to tell him that I was good at holding myself accountable and that he needed to find another partner. His tone made me believe that he wasn't going anywhere for a long time.

"Mya, right?"

"Uh...yes. What's your name again?" I asked, even though I never even knew it. Actually, I don't think I had even seen this man

before. Shows how much I pay attention.

"It's Aaron Journey."

I nodded as a response.

"Does everyone have a partner?" Mrs. Lamire yelled, which quieted the class. "Great! From this point forward, please get to know your partner, do weekly check-ins, and form friendships that you otherwise would not have. Does that sound like a plan?" Everyone just stared at her and a weak chorus of affirmations was mumbled. We all knew that we didn't have much of a choice. "See you all next week and have a great weekend!"

I got up to leave and started walking towards the door. I heard Aaron call my name from behind me and decided that I should at least act like I cared so I stopped to see what he wanted with me now.

"Shouldn't we exchange contact information? Wouldn't want a bad grade because we didn't do what she asked of us." He smirked.

"Sure. What's your number? I'll type it in my phone."

"Nope. What's your number?" He pulled out his phone instead.

I stood still for a minute because I could tell that he was on to me. "I'll type it."

25

He gave me the phone, I typed my number in, and he called the number as soon as he got the phone back in his hand. It rang and he said, "See you soon!" He winked and walked away from me.

"I'm sure he thought that was cute," I thought as I headed to my car.

A couple of hours later, I was sitting on my couch with Grace watching a psychological thriller - my favorite movie genre. I felt my phone vibrate with a text from an unknown number that said, "Hey. It's Aaron. I know you didn't save my number, so I am texting you to remind you to do that." After I saved his number, I let him know that it was saved.

I guess he was in the mood to text because he asked me what I was doing. I told him that I was watching a movie and he was distracting me. He apparently didn't care because he wanted to know what movie I was watching. He then asked me if I ever went to the movie theater. I told him that I didn't and that I was okay with watching movies at my house. My phone rang making me roll my eyes, but I slid my finger across the screen to answer it anyway.

"What if I wanted to take you to a movie? As an accountability partner, of course." He asked.

I laughed and said, "If you wanted to take me to a movie, you would ask and then I would tell you that I'd think about it and get back to you within three to five business days."

26

It was his turn to laugh. "Really? Well, partner, would you like to go see a movie? I'll even let you choose.

I smiled to myself as I responded, "I'll get back to you with an answer soon."

"I'll be looking forward to that." He replied softly.

I put my phone to the side and focused on my television until sleep overtook me.

My Saturday was pretty quiet. I went out for a morning jog, read, ate pizza, and watched The Office. Sunday, though, was slightly different. As a person who believed in God, I knew about the Sabbath day and Sunday used to be my day of rest. I used to read my Bible, pray, go to church, relax, clean, cook, and go to bed early. After Noelle died, and the more I dealt with my ever-evolving Meira issue, the further I grew from God. Church reminded me too much of my past with Noelle and I couldn't understand how God could take me through something like that. The death was enough, but now I had to deal with this girl in my mind that never went away.

This Sunday, I felt an unusual pull to do things that I usually wouldn't do. I realized that this was not my idea and was totally out of my control when I woke up extremely heated. It started off with me sitting straight up in my darkened room at around 5:00 in the morning. I didn't do anything, I just sat there for about an hour. I finally got up and started walking around my home praying loudly and speaking in tongues that I had never used before. During my pacing, I lost all awareness of what was taking place. Sometime afterward, I sat and thought about this empty space in my mind and I could not remember what happened during that time. When I finally came back, I looked at the clock and it was 11:15 am. I glanced at myself in the mirror and I was dressed in an old brown dress that I had had for years, I was extremely sweaty, and my hair was matted to my head as if I had just gone for a run at 2:00 pm in the middle of July. Even though I was aware of where I was and what was taking place, I still felt the strong and uncontrollable urge to continue the odd ritual. I would alternate between sitting in silence and then walk around and talk loudly with my hands outstretched. This went on for a couple of hours until I was able to regain control of myself and put a stop to this ritual. This had never happened before, so I was pretty shaken up when I realized that Meira was a lot stronger and had taken over my body for a while. I took the time to say a quick prayer, took a shower, and got back into bed.

The weekend was too short. I was sitting in Mrs. Lamire's class and she was asking if we had made contact with our partners over the weekend. Of course, the whole class responded by saying that they had. She started talking about regular classwork and we all diligently began taking notes.

At the end of class, Aaron stopped by my desk while I was packing up to ask how I was doing. I told him that I was fine and asked him the same question out of common courtesy. He told me that he was doing well but he would be doing even better if I would give him an answer to the question that he'd asked on Friday. I looked up at him and told him that we could go to the movies but only as accountability partners and friends. I jokingly told him not to get any ideas in his head. He chuckled and said, "Of course. Text me and tell me what movie you want to see, and I'll look up show times." I agreed to this and then we both went our separate ways.

The rest of my week was full of lectures, homework, quizzes, and group assignments. Aaron decided that we would go see the movie that I chose that Friday. I didn't feel comfortable telling him where I lived so we met up on campus, where I left my car, and he drove us to the movies. This was his great idea, not mine.

When we got there, I couldn't resist getting popcorn and an Icee. This always makes the movie better I told him. He decided to test my theory by purchasing two of each for us. The movie was great and right up my ally of psycho and thriller. I wasn't sure that Aaron liked it as much as I did. But when the movie was over, he told me the snacks definitely made the film better and that he really enjoyed spending time with me. He also thought that I was funny. "I think I'm pretty funny, too," I responded which made him laugh again.

On the drive back to my car, we listened to some music and when we reached my car, I told him that I appreciated the movie and snacks and that I would be willing to do it again. He looked at me for a moment and then asked, "What's your story, Mya?"

I could tell that he wanted to spend more time with me, but when conversations got too real, I usually chose to run. I sighed, and said, "I really wouldn't want to put a damper on this great night. You're my accountability partner, though, so I'm sure that you'll learn more about me as time moves forward." He looked at me and I could tell that he just wanted to know me, but I got out of his car and into my own. Back into a space where it was just me ... And Meira ... unfortunately.

Chapter 4

Present

    This was the first day since I was admitted to Goshen that I was actually looking forward to my meeting with Dr. Horia. At first, I wasn't interested in help. I had come to accept Meira and this whole convoluted situation as my new normal. I was sad for her in a way and almost felt guilty because she was going through this situation and not me. Right now, though, I was experiencing a little excitement at the thought of living a normal life again.

    When I made it to Dr. Horia's office, there was another person there. He was standing at the bookshelf and when he heard me, he turned around. He looked like he was in his thirties with brownish-red hair, a mustache, and a long beard, and at that moment as he greeted me, all my excitement drained away. The wall that had begun to crack was immediately built back in place.

    "Hi Mya, I'm Mike. I'm a minister here at Goshen and I would like to spend some time with you today."

    I just looked at him blankly.

    "I'm sure I caught you off guard. Dr. Horia had a family emergency and couldn't be here today, so I was asked to fill this slot of time."

    Still, nothing came out of my mouth.

    "How about you take a seat so we can chat."

I walked over to my usual seat and sat down even though I was pretty sure I knew what this conversation would entail.

"I am not here to force the Bible down your throat and I'm not here to lay hands on you." There went my theory of how this meeting would go. He continued, "I am simply here to share what is in my heart for you. I was walking around and praying before you came in and there were some things that were placed on my heart. Are you okay with me sharing them with you?"

I looked at him for a moment and then nodded in approval.

"Great. I would like to start by saying that I am not aware of your official diagnosis due to confidentiality matters. Also, there's no need for me to know." He paused a minute to grab his notebook off the desk behind him.

"So, to start, I felt the Holy Spirit share with me that there is a spirit of division within you." He almost said it as if it were a question. He continued, "Because I don't know you, I don't know exactly how this applies to your life. I was also told to share that certain things happen to chosen people. Because trials help us develop endurance, which develops strength of character. That character then strengthens our confident hope of salvation. And because God needs you to gain an understanding about some things that have happened in the past. Are these things making any sense to you?"

I couldn't do anything but sit and stare in awe at him. I knew exactly who was trying to get through to me and what was being revealed to me.

He went on by posing a question, "What is God developing you for or in you? What does He need you to gain an understanding about for you to move forward and out of your wilderness season?"

By the time he looked back up from his journal, I was crying. These were delicate and grateful tears because it had been such a long time since I had thought about God and His presence in my life. It had been a while since I had considered a relationship and intimacy with God for myself separate from Meira. Yet I had just received confirmation that God cared about me and it felt so good to feel this again.

Mike rushed over and knelt in front of the chair that I was sitting in. I looked him directly in his eyes and, as if I hadn't received enough confirmation in what he just shared with me, he said, "He cares about you." Those four words brought even more tears to my eyes in a way that I had never experienced. He continued to kneel in front of me and I could tell that he was silently praying while he waited patiently for my tears to stop.

"Would you like me to pray for you?" He asked.

"Yes." That was all he needed for him to come even closer, grab my hands, and start praying over me.

When the prayer was over, we both stood up and he gave me a big hug. Mike reminded me again that God cared for me. He also asked me if there was anything in

33

particular that he could pray for outside of this environment. I thought about this request and then I asked him, "Please pray that my heart will continue to soften, that my fiancé and I will be able to move past this hiccup in our relationship, and that I will be able to become whole again."

He smiled and said, "The way that you worded those requests sounds like you may know a little about the Word of God." I told him that I graduated from seminary school and he said, "Ahh, okay," as if it all made sense.

We talked a few more minutes about my educational background and then I left that office feeling and knowing that something had shifted within me. This was the start of a new beginning and a third chance at life.

4 ½ Years Earlier

"There is no possible way this man can be this perfect." I thought to myself as I stared stunned at Aaron standing at my front door with a huge bouquet of flowers and a card. I could see if it was Valentine's Day or even my birthday but nope. Today was his birthday.

About six months prior, Aaron had walked up to me and told me that he would be my accountability partner and our friendship had blossomed into so much more. I had never met anyone more patient, understanding, kind, funny, and handsome than him. At first, I was blinded by my situation, but as he persisted, I began to open up.

"Aaron, what are you doing?!" I practically squealed at him.

"I wanted to bring you something to let you know just how appreciated you are."

"But it's your birthday and I had some things planned for you to let you know how much I appreciate you and all that you've done in this short time." I stepped towards him, took the gifts from his hands, and gave him a big hug. "Thank you, Aaron. You are too good to me."

About three months into this friendship, Aaron and I decided that we would have a high level of transparency. I told Aaron about the traumatic loss of Noelle and how I had been coping. He shared that his mother had died a couple of years ago as a result of mental health issues that led to suicide. This amount of truth in our relationship propelled us into a deeper connection that, six months later, couldn't be broken. The only thing, though, was that I didn't tell him about Meira and what was happening in my head. I did plan to tell him sometime soon ... maybe.

"I am almost done getting ready and then we can go to destination one!"

He had sat on the couch while he waited for me to get ready and about 20 minutes later, we were heading to a brunch spot that I had chosen to begin his special day.

When we got there, we ordered mimosas and doughnuts, and

35

he questioned me about what was to come. I politely ignored that question and asked him how the mimosas were. From what I could tell, he was enjoying it.

An hour later, we had eaten, talking and laughing like we usually did, and I was driving us to his second birthday destination; a couple's massage. When we arrived, I told Aaron that we were getting "couple's massages." His face lit up and I knew that he was excited at the thought of us possibly being considered a couple. He had been questioning me about a relationship for a while now and I continued to remind him that I was not ready to go down that path.

After about an hour and a very relaxing massage, we were headed to our third destination. I knew that I was doing a lot for someone that I was not even in a relationship with, but he was becoming my best friend and he had opened my eyes up to so much in such a short time. He was also drawing my attention back to my relationship with God and His importance in our relationship. Aaron was such a wonderful influence in my life and there was really no reason for me not to move forward with our relationship. But my fear was that I may ruin it.

Our third destination, Pint and Pins, was a unique bowling alley where we could play different games, bowl, choose drinks from an open bar, and purchase full course meals. I had already reserved a lane for us so we checked in at the front desk and picked up our bowling shoes. While Aaron put his shoes on, I went and got us our favorite drinks to make this game a little more interesting and competitive.

After the game, which I won, we went back to the bar to eat some finger foods. I told Aaron that we needed to go to the store to get food and supplies to prepare for our pajama movie night.

Every time we went to the store together, we would disturb other customers with our childishness and this time was no different. As soon as we walked through those sliding doors, Aaron made the smart decision to cram his long body into the shopping cart and I condoned this act by pushing him as if it was normal.

The first thing we did was stop at the pajama section. Of course, he was wondering why we were in the men's section. I told him that I would be purchasing pajamas for the both of us. He shook his head but went with the flow. I chose blue, his favorite color, pajamas for the both of us.

Next, we went to the grocery side of the store where I picked up some raw chicken, ingredients to make cheese dip, some candy, and soda, which is what we chose to drink when we wanted to obliterate our health. I actually enjoyed having him in the cart because he wasn't able to pick up extra things or object to certain things that I picked up besides throwing a few things out of the cart like a kid.

After we left the store, Aaron dropped me off at my home with my new pajamas and he took the rest of our purchases to his home. I turned on some music, took a shower, and put on my pajamas. I also took the time to wrap Aaron's last major gift which was a nice watch that he had pointed out one time when we were window shopping at one of the local malls. I dropped this in a gift bag along with a special, handmade, and heartfelt card. This card was one of the most important parts of this day because I would finally give him some insight into how I felt about him. In the card, I wrote:

Dear Aaron,

I chose to give you this card at the end of the day because I wanted to save the best part for last and I knew that it would make you happy. Two things that I know you love are sentimental things and the truth and that is what this card entails.

I would first like to let you know how grateful I am for you. I have not been the easiest person to understand and it took me a while to open up to you, but you have stuck by my side. Since you came into my life, this is the most fun that I have had since Noelle died. Thank you for reviving a part of me that I never thought I would be able to experience again.

Thank you, also, for showing me what true friendship and love looks like. You are absolutely amazing, you are God-fearing, you are handsome, you are patient and kind, you have the best personality, and you make me laugh to list a few things. I could go on and on and make you cry, but I would like to finish by pointing out how many times you have spoken about us being in an official relationship over the past six months and I have decided

that I would want nothing more than to have just that.
Thank you for exceeding my expectations.

    Love Mya

When I got in my car, I sent him a text to let him know I was on my way so he could unlock the door. I hated to wait for him because there was always a weird man standing next door glaring at me. He told me that only a mother and her son lived next door, but I knew that a man was there every time I was there ... I think.

I made it to his house, parked, and began to approach the house when I saw something red on the outside of his door that looked like blood or paint. I opened the door and abruptly called out to him. Slightly frightened, I asked him "Is there something that I am missing?" He stared at me and I said, "The blood on the outside of your door."

He moved quickly to look at his door with a bit of panic in his eyes. He looked the door up and down and he said, "Mya, what are you talking about? There's no blood here."

I stepped back and huffed as if I was annoyed and said, "You don't see ... the ... there was blood here." I pointed and stuttered because I know what I had seen, and I also may have been starting to expose my inner conflicts. My mind automatically associated this scene with the time in the Bible where the Israelites were instructed to put blood on their doorposts to prevent death from entering their homes - the Passover. I knew that what I had seen was real, but it was not real in my reality. It was real in Miera's reality.

Embarrassed, I quickly started to stammer and told him, "Oh … sorry … it must have been the reflections from when the lights of my car were on and shining on the door. Let's go in and get the night started." I would not have Meira emerging and putting a damper on this beautiful night.

He was still looking at me in confusion, but I pushed his gift into his hand and walked past him into the kitchen. I finally heard the front door shut and he walked into the kitchen with a slightly happier expression. While I was preparing to cook, he sat on one of his barstools and started to take the card out. I stopped him and told him to open the gift first.

He put the card to the side and opened up the gift. He said, "Are you serious?! You did not have to get me this watch. Thank you so much, Mya!"

Next, he started to open the card and there was silence as he began reading. I was moving things around as a way to avoid the awkwardness of me just standing there waiting for him to finish. When he did, he looked up at me, stood up slowly, walked over to me, and gave me a big, long hug. This let me know that he loved the message more than he loved the watch.

He said, "So, just to hear it out loud, will you be my girlfriend?"

I looked at him, laughed, and said, "Really, Aaron? Yes." We hugged again and then we started cooking.

40

After the food was done, we found our places on the couch, turned on the movie, and ate. He chose an action movie which was his favorite genre and I actually found myself enjoying it and the delicious meal that we had made together.

When the movie was over, Aaron turned to me and said, "Thank you for this gift of the best birthday that I have ever had and thank you for making me the happiest man." I nodded and hugged him tightly. Let's see if he feels the same way after this ride starts rolling.

Chapter 5

Present

I had been praying that Dr. Horia would be available to speak with me today. The previous meeting with Mike went exceptionally well and I was very anxious to share these things and more with her. I also wanted to get some much-needed answers about what was going on with me internally.

I entered her office and let out an audible sigh of relief as I saw her sitting in her usual chair waiting on me to arrive. She looked up at me and smiled as she invited me to come in and take a seat.

"You're smiling today, Mya. This is my first time seeing you hold a smile."

"Even though last week with Mike provided me with some confirmations, I am very happy to see you today."

"Aww. Well, how are you?

"I'm better than I have been."

"What caused the shift?"

"Last week's conversation with Mike. He knew everything about me without even knowing me at all. He also gave me two questions to think about: 'What is God developing you for or in you? What does He need you to gain understanding about in order for you to move forward and out of your wilderness season?' I have been thinking about these questions and writing notes on random pieces of paper as thoughts would come up."

"Okay. Would you care to share what you came up with for those questions?" She asked.

I pulled out the scraps of paper that I had brought with me. "It's written really messy and incomplete, but I'll read a few of the things I wrote. So, for the first question, I wrote that I know that God is developing me for a future where I will be helping people, but I am not sure to what capacity or even where. I also know that He wants me to be healthy. For the second question, I wrote that He needs me to gain vision, knowledge, and wisdom. I am not exactly sure what that means at this point, but it's just what came to me. I am also not sure how my current situation will help with that, but I'm willing to see."

"This sounds great, Mya. I like that you chose to write this down. I believe that writing this out will help you track your progress, your thoughts, and your shift. Before we go any further and since you brought up writing, I have a gift for you."

From underneath her notebook, she pulled out a beautiful journal. I reached for it and looked at it for a minute. The cover was black and it had pink and gray writing on it that said, "My perspective is my reality."

I looked back up at her and all I could say was, "Thank you so much."

She then asked, "Do you know what that means?"

I knew that she was talking about the quote on the front of the journal. "Not really."

"Our reality can only be seen through our own perspective or lens. When our perspective becomes altered or our lens becomes cracked, our reality is distorted and that begins to be seen in our actions and behaviors. When that happens, we have to take the time to recalibrate, become self-aware, and correct how we envision the world to our liking or to what is acceptable. Ultimately, I believe that you should do what it takes to make your reality whole and complete. Spend time shaping your reality to be positive and one where you are not limited, afraid, or small. Does that make sense?"

"Dr. Horia, that was ... Wow. I completely understand what you're saying, and I am slowly but surely becoming aware that my reality is not what one would consider normal." I did air quotes around the world normal because what is normal really?

"You are an astounding and smart individual, Mya. Are you ready to dive into today's session?"

"Yes, ma'am!"

"So, let's start by discussing what you have been experiencing. I will first share what I gathered from what you told me at our last session and then you can give me feedback. This needs to be a collaboration. Is that okay?"

I nodded.

"Great. First, it appeared that you had been experiencing a second personality to whom you refer to as Meira. This second personality causes disruptions in your superior self and impacts your memory, behavior, perceptions, and thoughts. Second, you have previously experienced gaps in memory, more than once that you can remember, that is inconsistent with your normal memory patterns. Third, you have experienced significant distress in important areas of your life and daily functioning. Fourth, you have experienced disturbances that could be broadly classified as culturally or religiously abnormal. And lastly, your symptoms have not been caused by drug or alcohol abuse or any other medical conditions."

I followed every single word that she said, and I couldn't pinpoint one area as false. Everything was absolutely true and right on point. "This is all true." I replied to her with a serious tone in my voice.

She looked me directly in my eyes and said, "These symptoms are consistent with a disorder called Dissociative Identity Disorder. Have you ever heard of this?"

"I have. I had to study different disorders while I was in school, but I've forgotten most aspects of it."

"So, let's talk about it. Dissociative Identity Disorder, DID, or Multiple Personality Disorder is one that is associated with overwhelming or traumatic experiences and it can manifest at any age. Dissociation occurs when there is a lack of a connection between one's actions, thoughts, beliefs, memories, feelings, and/or sense of identity. It consists of an individual developing another persona or personality, having gaps in their memory which could also be referred to as a fugue state or reversible amnesia, and acting in an inconsistent way to one's normal behavior as a result of the disorder and not as a result of

45

drug or alcohol usage. Rituals, depression, mood swings, anxiety, panic attacks, and hallucinations are all symptoms of DID. In addition, 70% of people with this specific disorder have attempted suicide and other self-harming behavior is frequently reported. Is this making sense to you?"

"It is. Everything is starting to come together. Even though it's something that I never thought that I would have to deal with, it is a relief to hear an official diagnosis."

"One more thing before we talk about treatments. Your onset was more than likely caused by the traumatic death of your best friend. Also, you told me that in school you were reading through the Old Testament of the Bible. This is probably how Meira was formed in your psyche. That era of the Bible is fairly distant from the present day, which is your mind's way of trying to escape from this reality. It was also something that was at the forefront of your mind since you had been reading it. Does this make sense?"

"It does. The mind is a powerful thing, huh?" I asked this while shaking my head. It was pretty insane how the brain was able to do such unimaginable things.

"It most definitely is. Now, although there is no known cure for DID, there are some things that can help. Psychotherapy or talk therapy, Hypnotherapy, and Adjunctive Therapy are all helpful in the process of reconnecting your brain. I am not a fan of Hypnotherapy, but I am certified in Psychotherapy and Adjunctive

46

Therapy. For Psychotherapy, there will be quite a bit of talking as an effort to stabilize your real persona, Mya. Your family may be included in this if you would like. For Adjunctive Therapy, we will utilize Art Therapy to reactivate your coping mechanisms that were shut off when your traumatic event occurred. I know this is a lot of information, but I have everything in an official document for you. How do you feel?" She asked me this question as she looked up at me with true concern in her eyes. I knew that she wanted to do what it took to make me healthy again.

"It is a lot, but I'm taking it in."

"Okay, I haven't seen or heard you speak about Meira emerging in any way since you have been here, so I wanted to ask you if you still felt her."

"I do. I hear her. It seems like a calming effect has come over her."

"That may be due to the lack of triggering stimuli here in the hospital as opposed to the overwhelming number of triggers in the world outside of this building."

"Hmm. Interesting."

"Now that the hard part is out of the way, I need you to sign your treatment plan stating that I gave you all of the information about your diagnosis and further treatment." She handed the papers over to me.

I took a minute and scanned the documents to make sure that they were consistent with what she had just told me and then I signed. Then she said, "Lastly, homework. I want you to write a journal entry in your new journal

47

regarding how you feel about the information that you gained today and anything else that you may want to add. Please incorporate drawings, poetry, songs that may pop up in your mind, or whatever you may feel. I also want you to ask your parents about any mental health issues that they may have had or that they know of in your family. Does this make sense?"

"Yep!" I exclaimed. I stood up with my new journal and all of my documents, told Dr. Horia thank you, and left her office.

4 Years Earlier

I was so ready to get out of class and, even though Aaron and I were not in the same class, I knew that he was ready, too. We had a big weekend planned for my birthday and I couldn't think of anyone else that I would have wanted to do this with.

The instructor seemed to speak more than she ever had today. He went on-and-on about counseling theories and how we needed to find the best way to apply these. He gave us an assignment, stating that, "You must pick one theory and organize a counseling agency around it. Include training, modifications, cultural differences, marketing ideas, and the clients that you believe that you would be able to impact the most. This will need to be completed within the next two weeks. Also, this will be a group project. When I dismiss class, please locate your group members and exchange contact information with them." He finished his speech by walking around and handing out packets of information.

Of course, I did not want to work with a group of people, but I knew I had no choice. I didn't sit long before two girls, a tall, skinny, white girl and a shorter, Latina walked up to me and asked if I wanted to join their group. I told them that I didn't mind. I knew they approached me because I sit at the front of the class and get good grades. I think that some less motivated people can smell this.

The tall one, whose name I came to learn was Savannah, said, "We need to find one more group member," as she scanned the room looking for the next nerd. She laid her eyes on another black girl and said "her." She skipped right up to her and said, "We would like you to be a part of our group," as she pointed back at us. The girl shrugged and said that was fine. Our group now consisted of myself, Melissa, Savannah, and Raina. We all exchanged numbers and then left the class.

As soon as I reached my car, I called Aaron and asked him if he was on his way home to grab his bags. He told me that he needed to stop by the library to grab a book and that he would be at my house within the hour.

I made it home and told myself that I would finish packing right after I laid down for a 15-minute power nap. When I woke up, I heard a knock at my door and realized that my 15-minute nap had turned into a 45-minute snooze.

I jumped up quickly, opened the door for Aaron and rushed back to my room to throw the rest of my items in my travel bag. I had laid out quite a bit of jewelry to choose which pieces I would take with me, but I ended up sweeping all of it into the side pocket of my suitcase, throwing my last pair of shoes in the bag, and then rushing back to my living room to act as if I had it all together. We needed to leave by a certain time to catch our flight to Myrtle Beach, South Carolina and I was ready in time. As I tried to walk past him towards the door calmly, he said, "You fell asleep, didn't you?"

I just looked at him and said, "It was supposed to only be 15 minutes. My bad." We walked out the door and headed to the airport.

After about an hour and a half, we were seated in large, comfortable, airplane seats at the front of the cabin and were ready for our extended weekend on the beach. We had decided that I would plan something for tonight, he would plan activities for my birthday tomorrow night, and we'd both plan something together for the last two nights. I was definitely looking forward to our adventures.

When we finally landed around 4:30 in the afternoon, we decided to take a taxi to our resort since they were readily available at the airport. It took us about 25 minutes to make it to our temporary living quarters, but we were so impressed when we pulled up and even more mesmerized when we made it to our suite. We had a large living room area, a nice bathroom, and a huge bedroom. We also had a balcony where we could see the beach and all the way to the sun. It was absolutely beautiful. After being hypnotized for a few minutes by our view, I looked at my watch and realized that we had to be at the theatre soon, so I told Aaron to shower and put on something nice and I did the same. Because we were both into the theatre, plays, and the opera, I had done some research and found a show that would be taking place tonight. The reviews on it were great stating that it was a good show for tourists to enjoy.

Before we even went downstairs, I reserved an Uber and by the time we made it to the front lobby, he was pulling up. The venue wasn't far from where we were located so we were there early enough to take some pictures and then head in to get comfortable in our seats.

The show provoked many different emotions and had great musical pieces. It exceeded my expectations. I even considered leaving a review. Aaron told me, "This was a great start to our weekend," as we proceeded out the door and into another Uber. We paid our Uber driver a little extra to stop at a restaurant that we had ordered food from when we first got into the Uber, before dropping us off at our resort. We were both exhausted when we made it back to our suite, so we ate and went to bed.

We slept in the next morning and, around 10:30 am, Aaron woke me up singing happy birthday while handing me a small box. When I opened it, there was a beautiful, white gold bracelet with diamonds. I was so grateful for the gift that I almost cried. I did not expect him to get me anything because we had spent so much money on this trip.

Aaron told me to get up and get my swimsuit on because we were headed to the water today. Before I officially got up, I checked my text messages and there were a few happy birthday texts from my family and a few ladies that I met in some of my classes. I responded with a bunch of thank you text messages, let my parents know that I was having a good time, and got up to get dressed.

When we got to the beach, there were so many people and beautiful boats on the water. There was one in particular that was kind of just floating near the resort and it caught my attention because it was so glittery and fancy. I loved it. I told Aaron, "I would love to go on a boat like that one day."

"Well, let's go!" He grabbed my hand and we walked over to the boat. I told him that it wasn't the best idea to get on random boats and that I would rather not go up to strangers like this.

As we got closer to the boat, a man on board looked over and asked, "You two must be Aaron and Mya?"

Aaron responded, "We are." He stuck his hand out to shake the man's hand.

The man said, "For the next few hours, please take advantage of the mini bar, there are snacks in the refrigerator, and make sure you spend time on the front of the boat while we are on our tour to make sure you get some good views. How does that sound?"

"Great! Thank you, Mr. Sims." Aaron responded with a beaming smile.

When we went towards the front of the boat to put our things down, all I could do was drop my things and hug Aaron and then I said, "Why are you so amazing?"

He replied with, "Wait until we get to what's planned for tonight, baby girl." Once again, I wanted to cry.

The boat and tour were wonderful. I couldn't have asked for a better start to my birthday. When we stepped off of the boat, Aaron thanked Mr. Sims for the amazing time, and we walked to an empty area on the beach to sunbathe and enjoy the water for a while.

After about an hour or so, Aaron told me that we should head back up to our room to prepare for dinner. When we got back up to the room, there was a beautiful dress lying on the bed that he must have put there when he claimed to have forgotten his sunglasses and ran back up to the room right before we went to the beach. I just looked at him, but I couldn't find the words to express just how thankful I was for him, so I just said, "Seriously, Aaron?"

We got dressed, we danced, we drank a little bit of wine, and then we left the hotel room. Instead of going down to the lobby, Aaron pulled out a special key which took us up to the rooftop. When the elevator doors opened, I saw the ocean and the sunset which was captivating. When we walked out and turned to the right, there was a pallet, some soft music playing, a cabana, and covered plates and cups. He grabbed my hand and we walked towards the set up. I could no longer see because all of the tears that I held back.

throughout this special day were now pouring out. This was my physical representation of pure joy.

We both sat down on the pallet, Aaron prayed over the food, and we ate. When we were done, Aaron turned the music up slightly and we danced together until we grew tired. We laid down and talked for a couple of hours until we decided to go back to our room and get some rest. It was truly the best birthday I had ever had.

The next morning, Sunday, I woke up with a weird and well-known urge or push. All I remembered was getting up and walking towards my suitcase while Aaron was still asleep and then nothing else after that. A couple of hours later, I felt Aaron move which woke me up and when I looked at him, he was looking at me like I was crazy. He said, "Why would you throw all your jewelry on me while I was sleeping? What is wrong with you?" His expression portrayed utter confusion and irritation. I looked at him and then looked at the jewelry thrown all over the bed. At that moment, I knew that Meira had done this earlier when she woke me up and walked to my suitcase, so I had to think quickly.

I smiled at him to try to make it seem as if it was just a joke. "Remember in the Bible when the Israelites gave Aaron the gold to build the golden calf?" I put emphasis on his name because this was the best cover up that I could come up with to draw attention away from my emerging issue. He gave a half smile and said dryly,

54

"Oooohhh... You got jokes I see. You just couldn't wait until I was awake, though, could you?" And then he said, "Haha, you're real funny. At least I know that you read your Bible."

I was relieved that he fell for it and to take it a little bit further, I asked, "Since it's all here on display, what necklace should I wear today?"

He picked up a necklace that he always compliments when I wear it and said, "This one."

"Of course," I replied and started picking up all of the jewelry while silently cursing Meira in my mind.

Before we started getting dressed, we had to think about what today would entail. We decided that we would rent bicycles and tour the area where we were staying and then just spend time on the beach to eat, read, and relax. We got dressed and left. We found the station where the bicycles were held, and we started on our tour. Along the route, we found a wax museum that we thought would be interesting, so we dropped off the bikes and went inside where we spent more time than we had planned. Wax museums almost always creeped me out, but I couldn't help but observe every detail of the figures.

After we left, we got some food and then went to the beach. We stayed there a couple of hours before going back to our resort. For dinner, we ordered pizza and watched a movie in our room.

For our last day, we didn't have any set plans, we just knew that we wanted to relax on the beach and make sure all of our things were packed for tomorrow's flight back to Pennsylvania. We went to the beach, ate food, had a few daiquiris, and then laid around in the hotel room.

Before we knew it, we were walking through the airport to our gate slightly sad because we had to go back to reality. While we were seated and waiting to board, I told Aaron how grateful I was for this weekend and for him. He told me that he was grateful as well. He put his arm around me, kissed my forehead, and we remained cuddled until it was time for us to get on our plane.

In the past, I believed that most men, particularly black men, made it difficult to reach a certain level of love until I met Aaron. He reminded me that good, black men did exist and that everyone does not allow past negative and toxic relationships to cloud their judgement and impact their future. He helped me clear my perspective, or at least one of them.

Chapter 6

Present

After the last counseling session ended, I decided that it was time for me to contact Aaron. Before I dialed his number, I prayed that he would still be here for me after my bout of anger and the true revelation of my hidden battle. It rang twice and then I heard, "Hello?" It was Aaron's sweet voice.

"Hi, Aaron," was all I could get out.

He replied, "Hi, my love. How are you?" I beamed because I received confirmation that I was still his love.

"I'm doing much better." I replied.

"That's so good to hear. I've missed you so much."

"Aaron, I missed you, too. I want to apologize for my anger. I was not in my rational mind, but know I am grateful for what you did for me. Not only am I receiving answers about my mental situation, I am also getting communication from God."

He was quiet for a minute and then he said, "Why didn't you tell me the entire truth?"

I was also silent for a beat before I responded, "I thought that you wouldn't stay. I was afraid. You shared with me what happened with your mother and I didn't know if you would want to deal with that again."

"I understand that, but from the beginning we based our relationship on honesty." He sighed. "I also understand that this was one of the hardest things for someone to be honest about, though. Did you ever even consider telling me the full extent of your problems?"

"Every day, Aaron. I am so sorry. Will you forgive me?"

"Hmm. I don't know. Do you promise to love me and be honest with me forever?"

I giggled a little. He still knew how to give me butterflies. "Of course."

"Great, because we still have a wedding to plan when you get healthy."

I beamed. "I love you so much, Aaron."

"I love you, too"

For about an hour, I wanted to hear all about what he had been doing since I was away. He also wanted to know what I had been doing, my diagnosis, and my growing relationship with God. After the conversation was over, we planned for him to come visit.

Today was the day that Aaron and my parents were scheduled to come. I was so excited when one of the nurses walked into my room to tell me that I had visitors. I had on a yellow sun dress and I actually took the time to do my hair. I felt great about myself today.

When I walked into the big room, I saw Aaron, my mother, and my father sitting in the far right corner. I started walking towards them and, when Aaron saw me, he stood up and started walking towards me. I couldn't get to him fast enough so I ran and gave him the longest hug that I possibly could. We broke our hug and then I hugged my mother and father who also looked happy to see me.

"You look so beautiful, Mya." Aaron said.

"Thank you. How was the ride up here?" I said, looking at all three of them.

"It was pretty good. We talked about a lot including wedding ideas." My mom said with a huge smile. She may have been more excited for the wedding than I was.

"That's good to know. Dr. Horia gave me a new journal so I have been writing down some ideas as well. I'll share those when I get out of here."

"How is everything going?" My dad asked.

"Everything is so much better than it was. I now have a diagnosis. It is something called Dissociative Identity Disorder." I pulled out the many papers that Dr. Horia had given me and handed them to my mother."

While she was reading over them, my dad said, "This is great news, honey. I am glad we know what has caused all of this."

Then Aaron said, "Why don't you tell your parents about the Godly encounter that you had. I'm sure that would make them happy."

"I'm sure you're right," I responded. I told them all about Mike and the many confirmations that came to me in that time and even after.

After a two-hour long conversation, they told me that they needed to head back soon. As we stood up to say our goodbyes, my mother handed me a letter. She told me to read it carefully and that it would help me gain a deeper understanding about my family background. At that moment, I remembered that I was supposed to ask my

59

parents about their past mental health, but it was too late. I decided that I would call them before I met with Dr. Horia again.

Letter from My Mother:

To my beautiful and strong daughter,

I have decided to write you this letter to give you some insight into my background and to let you know that you are not alone in the battle that you are going through. Your mother understands more than you think.

As a child, my mother, your grandmother, was a very structured and strict lady. She had her ways, and she was stuck in them. When it came to me and my siblings, her way was the only way and if things did not go her way, she would "discipline" us. Sometimes, she would simply spank us with a belt or with a shoe. Other times, she would throw things, beat us, or hit us with the nearest thing she could get her hands on. She even threw a cast iron skillet at your Aunt Camilla for talking to one of the neighbor boys on the sidewalk in front of our house. You know how heavy and hard those things are.

When it came to things like church and God, she didn't want to hear about it. She said that Sundays were for cleaning, not for worshipping someone or something we can't even see, feel, hear, or touch. She would always say, "Everything I have, I earned on my own. It is up to you all to keep it all nice and clean."

As I went through grade school, I wasn't allowed to have friends and, if I did make friends at school, I was never allowed to bring them home. One time, a little girl named Denise got off the bus at my stop and walked home with me. When my mother saw that someone was with me, she treated the little girl so nicely and called her mother off of our landline. After the little girl had left, my mother was so angry that she locked me in a dark closet for the night. My siblings knew to never undo the punishment that my mother had done so they just sat outside the door and talked to me until we all fell asleep. I am assuming she forgot about me because she was looking for me the next morning.

When I was in high school, she got a boyfriend that was just as mean or even more so than she was. He would tell us what to do and we would have to listen. He had all the permissions that my mother had and that included yelling, throwing, beating, and whatever else he wanted to do to us.

One night, when everyone was asleep, I went down the hall to get some water. I think I may have made a little too much noise because that man followed me to the kitchen. I didn't even hear him when he snuck up behind me, grabbed me, and threw me outside. It was cold and rainy that night. I was dressed in shorts and a small shirt. As he walked back in, he said, "We don't kill mice, we just throw them out to their natural habitat," and then he shut the door and locked it. I was now on the back porch all because I wanted to get a drink of water. I assumed that he

61

wouldn't allow me to just stay out there all night, but he did. Somehow, in those conditions, I was able to fall asleep. I woke up to my mother jerking me up and telling me to "Get in this damn house before the neighbors see and call the people!" This was just one of the examples of the environment that I lived in with not one but two spawns of Satan.

When I went to the bathroom, I looked in the mirror and saw a beautiful girl staring back at me who I had never seen before. At that moment, I knew her name was Genene and I heard her say, in my mind, I am the one that will protect you. Turns out by "protect" she meant that she would get me in more trouble due to her careless actions, smart mouth, horrible judge of character, and lack of ability to make good decisions.

I went all through high school able to hide my pain. When I was at school, I was happy and excelling because school was my escape. No one ever suspected anything. When I was at home, I was getting in more trouble than ever because I was slowly losing control over this girl that had introduced herself to me not too long ago in the bathroom mirror.

Throughout this time, my guidance counselor at school was helping me apply for scholarships and make tough decisions about college. I had to think about how I would get there, where I would live, and how I would survive once there.

One night when I went home, my mother's boyfriend was extremely drunk. As the night progressed, he just continued to drink and become more belligerent. When I walked downstairs and tried to pass by him, he tried to get my attention. I ignored him because I knew that he was not in his right mind. When I didn't answer, he jumped in front of me, grabbed me, and yelled in my face, "You don't hear me talking to you, girl?!" I felt Genene emerging. My body tried to jerk away from his rough grasp and when I did, I am assuming he felt disrespected because he hauled back and punched me in my face. I completely blacked out and when I finally opened my eyes again, someone was picking me up off of the kitchen floor and another uniformed person was picking him up as well. I saw my mother and siblings standing around me with shocked faces. I had no clue what had happened. I just knew that it wasn't good. When we were in the ambulance, my sister rode with me and told me that she ran in on him slapping me and that by the time she made it to us, I had picked up a knife that was on the counter and stabbed him. She said that all she could do was rush to the phone and call 911. To make this story shorter, he died due to complications of the stab wound; his body went into shock at a quicker rate due to drug and alcohol abuse.

After this, my mother continued her evil reign until we all left the house. I didn't hear from Genene again until I was in my freshman year of college.

I had always been reserved, but when I was no longer under my mother's thumb, it allowed me to loosen up and have some fun. I didn't plan on doing too much, but

Genene planned on losing all of her inhibitions and all of my scholarships.

Genene pushed me to party all of the time. I would wake up some mornings in clothes that I didn't even know I had. I would wake up next to men that I didn't know existed. I had to go to the clinic plenty of times because I would end up with diseases and infections that, luckily, were all curable. People would speak to me and say things to me around campus that I had no clue about. One time, a man walked up to me and said, "I think I left my watch in your room." I was so confused and disgusted. Women started to judge me and give me ugly looks. I eventually stopped talking to my siblings because I was so consumed with these two lives that I was living. My grades were reflecting my behavior and I couldn't afford to lose my financial aid. I knew that I had to do something about this. I couldn't live like this anymore. The only good thing that happened during this time was that I had met your father. He didn't judge me, and he didn't talk to enough people to hear what was being said about me.

I started off talking to the school counselor. She was nice, she listened, and when she heard about what I had been going through, she referred me to a psychiatrist. Later that day, I set up an appointment with the psychiatrist and contacted your father to take me there.

This meeting was the beginning of the rest of my life. The psychiatrist asked me a whole bunch of questions, she asked about my past, she listened to my many stories including the one where I had killed a man without

64

showing one ounce of judgement on her face. She set up an appointment with me to come back so that she could share with me my diagnosis, causes, treatments, and more.

The next time we met, the psychiatrist was able to let me know that I had Multiple Personality Disorder. This was a shock to me because I had never even heard of such a thing. She told me that there was no cure for the disorder, but that she would be doing therapy with me weekly to reawaken the parts of me that had shut down and help me cope with stressful situations. She also told me that my other personality was more-than-likely birthed due to the trauma that I had experienced in my childhood home. Even though I was scared, I was at least grateful that I had answers.

For the next couple of months, I went to counseling, I started to excel in school, and I was no longer the talk around campus. I would actually have people come up to me and ask me where I had been or say that they thought that I had left school. I would just laugh and tell them that I was just focused on bettering myself. Some would laugh at me as if they didn't believe me and others would verbally express their happiness for me and even sometimes physically express that happiness with a hug.

Throughout this entire time, your father was there for me. He was here in a way that I had never experienced. We even went through trials where I tried to push him away before he could walk out of my life. He would always give me my space, but he would never leave.

One Sunday morning, he knocked on my door and told me that we were going to church. I don't even think that I had ever stepped foot in a church house, so I went just to see what it was about. We were a little late, so we walked into a crowd of students with their hands outstretched, eyes closed, rocking back and forth and side to side to the choir's singing and the band's instruments. To me, this looked like a trance. I was so tempted to walk right back out of that door, but there was something holding me down in my seat. It just so happened that on this specific Sunday, the pastor decided to talk about division within oneself, becoming whole, and understanding our purpose through our trials and tribulations. This completely shocked me because I felt as if the pastor was speaking directly to me. Your father had been the only one that I confided in, so I even suspected that he had set this up. That's just how hard the word had hit me that day and it also showed just how spiritually off I was at the time. At the end of church service when the pastor did an altar call, I was the first one to jump up out of the pew and walk to the front of the church. I didn't know what I was doing. I just knew that there was a strong pull to know who this God was that could intangibly touch me so deeply, so I went with it.

In a year, I had gone from being a wild child, a whore, alone in a room full of people, and being on the payroll for the enemy to someone who was intentionally living for Christ, focused, and truly connected with someone who I soon figured out was the love of my life and was put here for a huge reason. A couple of years after that, I had graduated, I was married, and I was living a great and fulfilling life. There were definitely many challenges and temptations along the way and sometimes I thought that it may have been easier to live outside of God's realm, but all I had to do was reflect, remind myself of where I was, and I realized that I didn't want it any other way. It's amazing the things that God can and will do once you give your life entirely to Him.

I decided the write this letter to you for multiple reasons:

1. It was too much to say and I wanted to make sure that I shared every necessary detail with you to let you know that your mother was not always a saint.

2. I wanted you to know that I understand what you're going through and, like me, I know you'll come out stronger on the other side.

3. I need you to understand the power of God. It's one thing to know His word, but it's another thing to have an intimate relationship with Him. He will be your strength.

4. Just like your father, Aaron is a great man. There were times that I did not cherish my husband as much as I should have, but God reminded me that He can take him away just as quickly as He brought him into my life. I got myself together.

5. *I needed to remind you just how amazing you are and how your story will be a testimony for the glorification of God.*

   You will make it through, and I love you!
   In transparency and honesty,
   Mom

Chapter 7

Present

I had written and drawn so much in my journal that it was almost to the point of being full. I wrote about my moods, my thoughts, my reconnection with Aaron, how I felt about my diagnosis, the things that God revealed to me, and my mother's letter which revealed a history of mental illness. I was ready to share all of it with Dr. Horia.

She greeted me as I walked through her office door and invited me to take a seat directly in front of her.

"How are you? She asked.

"I'm great, today. I have a lot to share with you."

"That's good to hear. I am ready when you are."

"I first wanted to start with the fact that my mother, in fact, was diagnosed with Multiple Personality Disorder when she was in college. It first developed when she was in high school and being abused by her mother. It was quite a dreadful but beautiful story. I am so proud of my mother." I decided not to tell her the extra details because that may have been too much for this counseling session.

"Interesting. How did that make you feel?"

"I feel even closer to my mother than I ever have. Her story let me know that I will get past this point in my life and be stronger than ever."

"Great."

"I also want to discuss my 'aha' moments. I'll read to you what I wrote:

After speaking with Mike, I chose to look at this experience in a spiritual way and attempt to decipher what God has been trying to reveal to me. The moment that I was able to see through the eyes of Meira, it seemed like something terrible at first, but then I realized that God was actually trying to reveal His character to me. I learned that He actually cares about His people.

When the people of the past went through those 40 years in the wilderness, it was not because God was just wanting to hold them hostage. It was because He wanted them to actually be obedient for their protection and so that they could be prosperous. He wanted them to understand what He had done for them, to stop complaining, and do what He needed them to do to glorify Him and get to the land of Canaan. I believe that we are sometimes held up in a wilderness stage because we are doing something that God has asked of us or we are not learning a specific lesson that He needs us to get before we move forward.

When it came to the Israelites in the Bible and Meira, God was perceived as someone who just wanted to make them suffer which was why they tried to revert back to what they knew: Egypt and false gods. Oftentimes, we do this. We don't believe that we are getting what we deserve from God, so we revert back to those temporary things that only provide us with temporary pleasures. Ultimately, I believe that this was a call back to God. I strayed as soon as Noelle died, and God knew that I would not come back to Him until I learned who He actually was and His purpose for my life. I don't believe that I am where I should be, but I am starting."

"Wow, Mya. You surely have gotten a lot from this stage of your life." She looked genuinely surprised and interested.

"I have!" I exclaimed excitedly. "And when it comes to my diagnosis, I realize that I have to do what is necessary to get better. I must be willing and open. I am ready to do what it takes to move out of this wilderness."

"That's so good to hear. We'll be starting the sessions specific to your diagnosis and healing next week. How does that sound?"

"It sounds like a plan. What will this entail?"

"It will include your family and fiancé - we will discuss coping mechanisms, those things that are sometimes hard to speak about. We will be attempting to shift your perspective and outlook to what you believe is acceptable and positive, and depending on where these conversations go, I will utilize what is necessary to address what comes up. How does that sound?"

"Like I said, I am willing to do what it takes. I know that you mentioned sessions where my family would be involved, should I contact them?"

"Umm. We won't be including them in the next session, but you can give them a heads up that this will be coming up in the future."

71

"Okay. I'll let them know the next time I talk to them. Does Aaron need to come since he is my fiancé?"

"I think that would be a good idea since he's a part of your support system. Is there anyone else that you will be inviting? I want to make sure to keep notes of this information."

"Possibly my Aunt Camilla. I'll contact her as well."

"The more support, the better. This type of therapy is very dependent upon collaboration, openness, emotions, and thoughts, so you can let your family know this information."

"Understood."

"Is there anything else that you would like to discuss?"

"Yes, you mentioned to me that Meira is contained because I am in this place with limited triggers. When I am released, will she come back?"

"Good question. By that time, I hope that you will no longer have the alternate persona and that you will be in tune with the proper coping mechanisms to utilize when you are faced with a triggering situation."

"Thank you. That gives me some hope."

"You're welcome."

I stood up to leave and before I reached the door, Dr. Horia reminded me that I am an outstanding person and to keep moving forward. I smiled and left.

There was a certain vibrancy to my field of vision. These glasses allow me to see things with a sense of gratitude and appreciation. One day, soon, they will be as vibrant as the Mike Myers "Cat in the Hat" movie.

3 Years Earlier

"Why don't you ever go to church with me?" Aaron asks.

In my mind, I think, "Please don't start this again." I turn to him and say, "Aaron, I have already told you that I will eventually go to church with you when I am ready."

"Yes, but you never explained to me why you turned away from church. You told me that you and Noelle would go all of the time."

"We did." I started to feel something well up inside of me. I sat down on the couch and put my face in my hands. I didn't want to think about this or anything that could bring back those precious and beautiful memories that now caused me pain.

"I'm sorry. I just want you to experience life abundantly." He sat down beside me.

"Aaron, I am not ready." I told him in a barely audible voice.

He sat for a second longer, said "I understand," and got up to do some things that didn't even need to be done.

I laid down on the couch, caught up in thoughts, and drifted off to sleep. With Noelle fresh on my mind, I had quite the dream:

We were sitting on the porch of our old, now cremated, home laughing and talking. She looked over at me and said, "What's going on with your face? It's ... changing."

I reached my hands up to touch my face and something felt odd. It felt like melting tar. I rushed into the bathroom to look into the mirror and it was the distorted face of Meira.

She started cackling and then chanted, "Turn away, disobey, we'll never make it to Canaan anyway." It was getting louder and louder and her face in the mirror began to get even more distorted until it turned into the face of what some would describe as a demon.

I could hear Noelle banging on the door to the bathroom door, trying to get in and stop the incessant chanting. There was chaos, the room had adopted a red hue, and, in the mirror, I could see people behind me, chanting that same saying over and over with Meira. They had no facial features except for huge mouths that covered up half of their faces.

All at once, I fell to the floor which was made of sinking sand, the screaming and the banging stopped, and I heard a low whisper that said, "Cross over the Jordan River." I felt power come back into my body, I stood up, looked back into the mirror where I saw Aaron with Noelle standing a distance behind him.

When I opened the door to the bathroom, I was in the modern church where we had Noelle's funeral service. It was full of people with their hands outstretched towards me, and I couldn't stop my legs from walking to the altar. The pastor standing in front of me was a man that I had never seen before and he was constantly moving his hands in a motion that was telling me to keep walking towards him. I kept walking, but I was getting extremely tired. Eventually, I fell to the floor and fell into a deep sleep.

I jumped up from my weird dream as soon as my head hit the floor of the church and called out for Aaron. When he came out from the kitchen, he immediately looked concerned when he saw my face. He said, "What's wrong?" I told him about my dream, he said "wow," and we sat there on the couch.

I then said, "I'll go to church with you."

He looked at me and said, "Are you sure? You don't have to if you aren't ready." I told him that I was sure. I almost felt like I had no other choice.

Sunday morning, I threw on a casual dress, pulled my hair into a sleek ponytail, and put on some mascara and matte lipstick. Aaron arrived at my home at about 10:15 in the morning so we could make it on time for the 11:00 service. I didn't say much to him when he walked into my home. It wasn't that I was upset with him, it was just that I felt as if I was being pulled into a mental space and sort of forced to think about the past. Also, the dream was still on my mind.

We made it to the church and were greeted by a diverse group of people who were extremely friendly and handing out brochures with church information on them. We found a seat right in the middle of this humongous sanctuary. He turned to me and said, "We can leave at any moment that you feel out of place. I truly appreciate you for being here with me today." I smiled and grabbed his hand as a way to let him know that I was grateful for him.

A few minutes later, everyone in the church was up on their feet and wholeheartedly participating in praise and worship. Aaron had his hands uplifted and he was singing along with the songs. I, on the other hand, felt slightly disconnected from what was taking place around me.

Once we were instructed to take a seat, a few people walked on stage, multiple announcements were made, an offering took place, and there were a few prayers done. Finally, the lead pastor came on stage and greeted everyone. He dove right into the message for the day and it took Meira no time to find her way to the forefront of my perception.

Right then, the entire building around me began to turn into a grayscale and cool tone. I looked around me and noticed that everyone's skin began to change to a darker brown color even though the congregation was highly diverse in races. As I continued to listen and focus on what was taking place, the pastor's voice began to deepen, his words began to slow down, and then I realized that I could no longer pinpoint certain words that he was saying. When I looked up, he was a completely different person, and he was speaking a different language that I had never heard before but that I completely understood. I turned to look at Aaron to see if there was at least one thing that was familiar here and he was no longer the Aaron that I was in a relationship with, but Meira knew this person was Aaron, Moses' brother. I knew that this couldn't be real, but I couldn't help but jump up to my feet and run out of the church. Between the time of my exiting the church doors and Aaron stopping me in my tracks as I was aimlessly walking down the road shoeless, I had no clue what had happened.

"What happened back there?!" He was almost yelling. I couldn't answer. Up to a certain point, I knew that Meira shifted my reality to hers.

"Mya?!"

"What, Aaron?! I am sorry. I tried to tell you that I was not ready. And even though I did not feel forced by you, I still felt dragged to church. I took the dream as a sign to go to church."

He sighed deeply and said, "Where are your shoes?"

"I don't know. I don't really remember losing them."

"Do you want me to go back and find them?"

"No, I want to go home."

Aaron drove directly to my house without another word. When we got there, I got out of the car halfway expecting Aaron to follow me into my home. When I looked back, right before I unlocked my door, he was backing out of the parking spot and driving away. A deep feeling of sadness washed over me.

For the next few days, I expected Aaron to reach out to me. I had so many thoughts from both myself and Meira. I kept asking myself if I had blown it with Aaron or if I should just forget about the relationship. I even thought about coming clean about everything that was going on with me. Those negative thoughts were appreciated by Meira and the thoughts about coming clean to Aaron were combatted by her. She wanted to make sure that her agenda and purpose was first in my life. Why couldn't I defeat these thoughts? Why did I keep allowing her to win?

About a week later, I received a call from Aaron. He asked if he could come over and I told him that he could. He sounded...different. To pass the time and not allow my mind to wonder about what Aaron would say to me, I cooked for us. I decided to make lasagna with green beans and then I ran to the store to pick up a bottle of wine. I guess I also felt slightly guilty about what had happened. Aaron really wanted the best for me and I was making this relationship so hard for him. I knew the importance of having a relationship with God, but I also knew that something, or someone, was standing in the way of that. I just couldn't bring myself to reveal that truth. I was too fearful of her, his reaction, and of being alone again.

That night, when Aaron arrived, he gave me a big hug as if he was happy to see me, but his facial expression told a different story. There was dissonance. I gave him his plate of food, we ate, and then we both took a seat on the couch. Everything seemed pretty awkward.

Aaron first asked me how I was doing. After that, he proceeded to tell me why he hadn't reached out to me like he usually would have. He admitted to me that he felt as if I was not telling him everything about myself. I knew that this would happen. I knew that I should have told him about Meira a long time ago. I clammed up and was unable to respond to what he was saying to me. In my mind, I clearly heard, "I will not allow you to say anything to him about me. He will try to get rid of me."

He sat for a minute longer before he said, "Do you have nothing to say? What is your problem? I know I shouldn't take this personally, but it's starting to feel like you don't trust or want to talk to me. Have I made you feel like you can't be open with me?" He was getting worked up.

"No, Aaron! There are just some things that I don't know how to explain ... or am afraid to explain... or just can't." My words were starting to come out as a jumbled mess.

"Afraid of what?! What have I done to make you afraid?"

"Nothing. You haven't done anything!" I feel like I can't get my words out quick enough before he stands up. The situation was escalating quickly.

"Okay. Since I am not the issue, this must be something that you need to handle on your own and I am willing to give you the space to do that."

The tears were welling up as Aaron started taking those steps towards my front door to leave. I had never seen him like this. Was it stress? Anger? Sadness? Disgust? Why couldn't I stop him? Why couldn't I tell him the truth? Why couldn't I just calm this situation by giving him deeper access to my life? I kept telling myself to speak, yell, squeak, something. I couldn't. The situation was out of my hands.

Aaron turned around once more, looked at me and said, "Nothing? You have nothing to say?"

I couldn't even respond after seeing the amount of hurt that I had caused him. I couldn't respond to stop that hurt from even happening in the first place.

Aaron opened the door and walked out.

Chapter 8

Present

"Hi, Mya?" One of the assistants peaked her head into my room as if she expected me to be naked. "Dr. Horia called us to let us know that she had to take an unscheduled and emergency break. She will not be here for the next couple of weeks. She wants you to utilize the art area of this facility to expound upon those ideas that come to you. She also needs you to continue writing in your journal. You can also request to meet with Mike if you ever feel the urge to do so. We're also here for your support so please let us know if you need anything."

She waited for me to respond, but all I did was nod. I felt down as soon as I heard her speak those words. I needed to continue this positive progression and Dr. Horia was my closest form of support. I decided, though, that I would maintain my positive path and not let any distractions in. I would meet with Mike once or twice, and I would do what Dr. Horia told me to do at this time. I also prayed that she would see my amazing progress when she got back, and she would go ahead and sign the papers for me to be released from the hospital. And I had already made up my mind that she would be my therapist once I was back into the real world if that was possible.

For the first week without Dr. Horia, I read, I went to the art room, I talked to my family quite often when they weren't visiting with me, and I even met with Mike. Our second meeting was even better than the first. We prayed together, listened to praise and worship music, talked about God's Word, and we even decided that he would be my spiritual mentor because he felt that the Holy Spirit was speaking this to him. I was still progressing without Dr. Horia here and without being controlled by Meira … or so I thought.

The next Sunday, there was a knock on the door to my room. I looked up from my notebook as the door began to open. Standing in front of me was a young lady about my age. She was quite beautiful, but there was a certain scruffiness about her that I couldn't quite pinpoint. She also looked extremely familiar to me, but when the database of my mind couldn't locate her, I let it go.

"Hi. Are you Mya?" She sounded so sweet but so familiar.

"I am. And you are?"

"I am Ahlai. I am sorry for disrupting your quiet time. I was just told to come in here and put my things down." She said this as she began walking to the empty bed located on the opposite side of the room.

"It's no problem. So, you'll be my new roommate?"

"That's what I have been told. I have been here for a while, but my old roommate needed to be isolated for some reason, so they moved me."

"Okay. I haven't seen you here before, but maybe that's because I tend to stay to myself as much as possible." I giggled to soften that statement.

82

"I have definitely seen you before. I am pretty sure that you and I came in around the same time."

"Oh. Good to know. So, what brings you here?" I said this in a way to where it didn't seem like I was trying to pry information out of her.

"Well, honestly, I had a mental breakdown. I was in a dark space for a long time. It felt as if I was wandering for years and years with no end in sight. I was admitted here when I tried to end my life. I was so tired. What about you?"

I don't know why I asked her that when I knew I wasn't ready to talk about it myself. I just responded with, "I had a terrible bout of depression after a traumatic situation."

She looked at me as if she knew I was lying and then she said, "We all go through those times, right. I am just hoping that we can get out of here soon."

We? What does my situation have to do with her? Why does she seem to be so concerned about me? Maybe I'm just overthinking what she said. I looked back at my journal and said, "Yeah. I hope."

Over the next few days, I actually grew sort of fond of her. It was bound to happen since we had to wake up and sleep near one another every day. We also seemed to be on the exact same schedule. Everywhere I was she was also there. With this fondness grew a level of trust so when she would ask me if I wanted to explore something or do something with her around the hospital, I would. I assumed she did this on her own time as well.

83

One particular Sunday, Ahlai told me that she wanted to show me something and that it was important. I told her to hold on a moment while I gathered myself and threw on some decent clothes. Once I got myself together, she took my hand and led me down the hall, we turned right onto another hallway and then we took another right turn where I saw one of the janitorial workers that I would speak to everyday. She spoke to me cheerfully and didn't even acknowledge Ahlai. I assumed that they had never met one another, but I didn't feel like introducing them, so I spoke back and continued on my way. We soon stopped at the third door on the left. I assumed that all of these doors were rooms for other residents here so, at this point, I figured we were going into someone else's room that she had met.

As we were approaching the door, I was thinking about how I wasn't sure if I could trust this girl or why I was even going along with her when she gave me such a weird feeling sometimes - just like the feelings that were happening right now. When she went to put her hand on the doorknob, she abruptly paused and stood there for a minute as if she heard my thoughts. I felt a wave of heat hit my body that I hadn't felt in a long time. Right then, she turned to me with an unnerving look in her eyes and said, "I.... I just forgot that I needed to meet with one of the other girls that I met earlier today. Sorry I brought you all this way. Maybe I can show you another time?"

Something was so off about her and she looked so disturbed. What was it? What happened in just that short moment that made her turn icy cold? I just couldn't put my finger on it or on why I felt like I knew her, but I just relied on the thought that this was why she was in a mental health hospital. I replied with, "Okay. That's fine. See you later." I walked back to the room without even glancing back at her. My mind was going through the many thoughts attempting to place her and process what just happened. What was that look?

The next week, Dr. Horia was finally back. I was excited to meet with her and tell her about the new friend and roommate that I had. She first took the time to apologize and let me know that she had had a family emergency. She appeared to be tired, but, nevertheless, she was still enthusiastic and ready to start today's session.

She started off our talk with, "So, tell me what's new? What has changed since I have been gone?"

"Well, I feel like I have still been progressing and positively moving forward. I have been writing, talking with my family, and praying. I also met with Mike who provided me with even more confirmations. I really think that I am at the end of my time here."

"Okay. I see."

"I also met someone else. She came in at the same time as I did. She is my new roommate and we have actually become pretty close over the last few weeks. She is really nice and very open about her situation which encourages me to also be open."

"Well, sounds like you have told me everything except her name." Dr. Horia said this expectantly.

85

"Her name is Ahlai Foe. I assume you know her since you are the main therapist here and you have to know all of us."

"Hmm. I don't think I recall that name, but there are some instances where I don't immediately meet you all. Why is she here?"

"She told me that she attempted to commit suicide after some sort of mental breakdown. I guess it's kind of similar to my situation." I was trying to be a little more open when it came to this subject and accept what happened so that I could make changes.

"Gotcha." Dr. Horia stood up, walked around her desk, and took a seat at her computer desk. She had a weird look on her face while she was typing in some information, reading, typing a little more, reading, and then pausing. "Mya, you said her last name was Foe like F-O-E?"

"Yes, is something wrong?"

"How do you spell her first name?

"It's A-H-L-A-I." I was getting a little annoyed because I wasn't sure what she was doing. She stood up, walked back over to her chair that was positioned directly in front of me, sat on the edge and said, "Mya, I will do a little more investigating, but we do not have nor have we ever had a patient or an employee here by the name of Ahlai Foe. You have spoken before about discernment so, in this situation, please utilize it."

2 Years Earlier

I went to class, went home, did my homework, slept way more than I should, mentally communicated with the girl in my head, sat on my couch, in an endless loop. This was how my days were going. I was going through the motions - class, home, homework, sleep, Meira, acting like everything was normal in my life. It was the same old, tiring cycle. I had also mastered the appearance of what I thought was normal. I smiled at people, attempted to form connections and interactions, I went to parties, I even went on a few dates. The good part was that this was a great distraction. The bad part was that this was a great distraction, and it was all only a façade.

After the church debacle that happened about a month ago, Aaron decided to step away from my life. I was angry at first because I felt like he was leaving me when he knew that I was struggling with something. Then I thought about it. How could I be mad at him when I couldn't even be honest with him and when I allowed the fear of what could happen to control my actions to the point of losing? Either way, I took my losses and, even though I felt the void of him not being in my life, I pushed forward the best way I knew how. I thought plenty of times about contacting him, but I guess I could say that it was either pride or a relief of not having to be honest with someone. So, for a month, I had not heard from Aaron, seen Aaron on campus, or heard about him. I was okay as long as it stayed that way.

During this time, Meira's reign of terror in my life began to expand. For one, when I was on my cycle, she had started calling me ceremonially unclean. That also came with purification ceremonies and things that I had no control over. I had previously read about the many purification ceremonies that God instructed the Israelites to do that included sacrificing animals and isolation. Unfortunately, those purification ceremonies got pretty serious. I am just grateful that no one ever caught me in the midst of performing one of them.

One night, I woke up around 11:30 due to horrible cramping. I climbed out of my bed to take some medication knowing that these cramps would only continue to get worse. I was also extremely hot which usually only meant one thing - Meira's strong presence. I got back in bed to try to force myself to quickly fall back asleep and I did. Before I drifted, I said a quick prayer because I just didn't have a good feeling about what was to come.

When I woke up, the entire front of my shirt was covered in a red substance along with my hands and there was this same substance splattered all over my legs. There was also something that appeared to be mud mixed in with the blood-looking matter. After a minute of being baffled, I jumped up and ran to the bathroom in a panic because I wasn't sure if I had gotten shot or if I had been stabbed. I quickly took my shirt off and realized that there was nothing on my body to indicate from where this blood would have come.

I walked out of the bathroom and towards my living room to grab my phone from where I had left it the night before, but something caught my attention in the kitchen. I slowly turned around and paused at a distance to attempt to gather myself before willing my feet to move in the direction of the kitchen. When I finally gathered some courage, I walked into my kitchen to find blood covering my kitchen counters, a knife covered in blood, and a dead, burned-to-a-crisp cat on my stove.

I stood completely stunned at the horrific scene that was in front of me and I thought about Grace, my puppy. The only good thing was that this was not her on this stove. On the other hand, I instantly knew that Meira had done this and as soon as that thought surfaced, she confirmed it by letting me know just how ceremonially unclean I was and how last night she performed a purification ritual before my seven days of isolation. Seven days of isolation?! I had class and I had things that needed to be done. I couldn't remain isolated for seven days and I wouldn't. As soon as I thought that she shot back a rebuttal by letting me know that she was in control and that I would not be going to class. I thought, "We'll see about that," as I took a few steps forward to see just how bad the disaster before me actually was.

It took me all Sunday to clean my home. Even though most of the mess was in the kitchen, Meira had tracked dirt and blood all through my home. This meant that I had to deep clean the kitchen, the bathroom, my bedroom. I had to sweep and mop the floors and vacuum and shampoo the carpet. She got in my bed and made me sleep in the blood of a dead animal which made this process that much more difficult. I was also battling fatigue and cramps the entire time. By the time night had fallen, I was so tired. I went to bed ready to get into a new week and start fresh. I chose to block out any deep thoughts or fear about what I had just experienced.

When morning came, I was still not feeling my best, but I got up to get ready for school anyway. I got dressed, gathered all of my books together, and was getting ready to head to my vehicle when I suddenly felt a jolt in the opposite direction of the front door. I dropped all of the items that I had in my hands and couldn't stop myself from walking until I had made it back to my bedroom and into my bed. The whole way back to my room, I was attempting to grab onto doorways and pieces of furniture to stop her from dragging me, but I couldn't. As hard as I tried to get up and move, I couldn't. There was a heavy weight on me that I could not lift. Right then, I remembered Meira telling me that I would have to be isolated for a week due to the fact that my cycle was on and I was "ceremonially unclean."

For an entire week, I missed my classes, but I was not going to let Meira make me entirely irresponsible. I emailed my instructors to let them know that I was ill and I texted a few friends and asked them if they could send me any notes that they had taken in any other classes that we had together.

I was so frustrated. I started to cry because this was too much. That situation should have propelled me right to a counselor's office as soon as Meira would let me go, but, for some stupid reason, I still did not go to counseling. I knew that I should have, and something even told me that I eventually would, but Meira continued to remind me about how that would have been a bad decision, how she believed that she was helping me, and that other people would not accept me or help me as she was. In my own mind, I had my own fear because now, I was the epitome of a beginner serial killer and I had no clue what people would think about me. I was not ready to face the truth.

Chapter 9

Present

Ahlai was a gnat. She was with me all of the time. She talked all of the time. She knew way too much about me that I had never communicated with her. When she would slip up and say things that I never told her, she would tell me that I did tell her. When I would think certain things, she would immediately react like she knew what I was thinking. What was this girl? She also claimed to be a Christian so she would talk to me about the Bible. The problem was that it seemed as though she only read Exodus, Leviticus, and Deuteronomy. She was almost obsessed with the wilderness journey of the Israelites. That was interesting to me because that specific wilderness journey was what almost caused me to lose my life thanks to Meira.

"Are you listening to me, Mya?"

"Uh, yes. I was listening."

"Okay. So, what do you think about it?"

"About what? Remind me."

She rolled her eyes. "What do you think about us taking our own personal journey through this hospital? We can stop at certain places and think about what it may have been like to experience the golden calf or the people getting punished by God for sinning against him. I think it would be cool to put ourselves in their place."

I paused for a long while just looking at her. I just couldn't imagine that she could be serious about something like this. What kind of sick journey would that be? Why would it be acceptable to recreate those hard times?

Then she said, as if she read my mind, "This would be so that we could understand why God did the things He did or even why the Israelites did some of the things that they did."

Yep. She was most definitely obsessed. This was abnormal. "Let me think about it. For now, though, I think I'll just write in my journal and relax."

"Fine by me. I think I will go through the wilderness on my own. You are so boring." She was mad, but I didn't care. I just turned away and started writing about her hoping to make some sort of connection about this girl. I wrote in my journal, read my bible, listened to some music, and eventually, I fell asleep.

In the middle of the night, I was awakened by someone chanting or speaking in tongues. When I squinted my eyes to see what was happening, I saw total darkness except for a small light in the middle of my room and Ahlai sitting right in front of it rocking back and forth. The problem was that she was facing me and she had her hands outstretched towards me. Her eyes were closed so she wasn't looking at me. I was pretty nervous about this. I turned over in my bed as if I was still asleep, she paused, and then she continued that weird talking when she assumed, I was just readjusting in my sleep. I stayed up for as long as I could, but I said a quick prayer and went back to sleep. I knew this girl had mental issues, but I also knew that she couldn't hurt me because, well, we were in a hospital. I apparently forgot that harm can be a mental thing as well.

The next morning, I got up and thought about what I had experienced last night. I looked over at Ahlai's bed, but she was not there. As soon as I did this, she walked into our room carrying breakfast. As if this were a five-star hotel, she walked over and brought me a bagel, yogurt, and a banana. "You were sleeping so peacefully so I didn't wake you up to get breakfast." She smiled so sweetly, and I just knew that what I saw the night before couldn't have been real. I stopped thinking about it and politely ate the food that she brought me.

When we were both done eating, we talked for a while and, of course, the conversation went back to the Bible so, to stop her from going on and on about this, I thought that I would bring up a previous situation. A while back, Ahlai mentioned that she needed to show me something, but when we approached the door, her demeanor changed, and she made up an excuse as to why she needed to leave. Out of curiosity, I asked her, "Do you remember when you were going to show me something and you took me to that door a couple of halls over and then stopped because you needed to meet someone?" When I said that last part, I thought about how I had never even seen her with anyone else. I wondered who this person was for a brief second.

94

"I do."

"What happened to that? What was it?"

"Oh. I assumed you didn't care anymore so I just forgot about it."

"We really don't have much to do right now so I would like to know what it was."

She hesitated and then she looked at me as if she were questioning whether or not I was serious. "Are you sure?"

Now it was my turn to hesitate. "I guess. I didn't think it was a big deal. What could you possibly need to show me in this hospital where everything is blocked off to make sure that we don't harm ourselves?"

She got up from her seated position and started walking towards her shoes which were worn down the back and said, "Well, come on then. Put your shoes on so we can go back over there."

"Is it still there?" I only expected her to tell me what it was not to attempt to show me again.

"It's still there. It will always be there as long as I have something to do with it."

What a weird comment. I couldn't imagine what she could have possibly been talking about especially if she was in control of it. "Umm. Okay." I responded as I got up, threw on some decent lounge clothes, and stepped into my slippers for our walk.

We ended up taking the exact same route as last time and, this time, I tried not to think much about it and go with the flow. When we arrived at the exact same door, she turned to me and asked, "You ready?"

I was almost frightened at the smile that came across her face, but I said, "Yes."

She opened the door, pulled me in, and shut the door all in one swift motion as if she didn't want anyone else to see what was in there. It just looked like a regular, underutilized room. And I said, "Well, where is it, Ahlai?"

With that same smile, she tightly snatched up my hand and dragged me to the farthest window where she pointed and told me to take a look. When I shifted my glance from her to the window facing the outside world, I was in total confusion. I saw people walking towards us; thousands and thousands of people. They looked hot, exhausted, and hungry. There was a big mountain in the far distance that I noticed because the line of people extended almost all the way back to it. As the people got closer and closer, there was a smell of must in the air and there were sounds that I couldn't quite make out. They were getting closer and it sounded like the people were complaining and griping about being thirsty, tired, and going back to Egypt. Egypt?! My thoughts began to rush around my mind, my head began to pound, and my temperature began to rise with great intensity, but I could not look away from the scene that was unraveling in front of me.

Next, all I saw was a flash of light and I jumped back. When I looked back at the window there was chaos and fire. The most shocking part was that there were a number of people who were set on fire and the people around them were screaming the name of someone. Whose name were they saying? I turned my ear to be able to hear them and they were saying … Moses. When they called the name of Moses, there was an audible prayer that I could hear asking God to stop the fire, and as soon as the prayer was done, the fire stopped. At that moment, I remembered this exact scene from the Book of Numbers in the Bible. It occurred while the Israelites were in the wilderness with Moses as their leader, but I couldn't understand why I was seeing this. I was in the hospital getting better. What was happening to me?

I looked over at Ahlai to ask her what she had done to me and with that same conniving smile, she said, "Oh, Mya, you stupid, stupid girl. Didn't you know that when you lived, so did I? I told you to stop putting other people before me and you just wouldn't listen. Ha! Look at your face. You really thought I was gone, didn't you?"

"Wh…what? What are you talking about? You were supposed to be …" I stopped abruptly because it all hit me like a freight train. I know that it should have registered a long time ago, but I finally knew exactly who this girl was, and I needed to get away from her immediately. I must have been too overwhelmed and too disoriented because complete blackness consumed me and, seconds later, I felt the hard cold floor beneath me.

1 Years Earlier

Graduation was finally right around the corner and I was totally ready. I had great grades and I even had some good job opportunities waiting for me, but I was as far away from who I thought I should have been as the East was from the West. I successfully programmed myself to act how I believed a normal human being should act. I incorporated different aspects into my behavior that I copied from the people I surrounded myself with; the way I laughed, the way I said certain words and phrases, flirting, gossiping, drinking, and being all around superficial and vain.

A little while ago, I finally broke down and contacted Aaron. The first thing I said when I heard him say "hello" over the phone was, "Please give me time and I promise that I will open up." I was at my most vulnerable and I couldn't imagine being that vulnerable with anyone else except him. We still kept our space, but I could tell that he still truly cared. He told me that he chose not to entertain any other women because God told him that I was the one for him. He kept hearing the word "patience" over and over. He was obedient. Aaron and I continued to talk every day. We were almost back to where we used to be and we would hang out sometimes. We also eventually started saying "I love you" again, but I could still sense that he was a little distant and I knew why.

This specific day, I knew that I wanted to tell Aaron everything, but I just wasn't sure how I was going to bring myself to do it and rebel against Meira whose power was insanely strong these days. I thought that joining the girls that I hang out with on their hiking trip would be a great way to clear my mind and be able to think clearly. Telling someone these details was a big deal and I wanted to prepare myself.

There were five of us going on this trip. Savannah who was the slender, tall, and fit one had initiated this trip. Melissa who was the short, tanned, firecracker who often had issues because she was too friendly with men and not friendly enough with their girlfriends. Then, there was Raina who I was closest to - she was a little taller than me, a little darker than me, and she had beautiful, natural hair. I had met them all through a group assignment in one of my classes and we just continued to hang out after that class ended. The good part about this group was that it was diverse with me and Raina being black, Melissa being Latina, and Savannah being white. The bad part about this group was that everyone talked about everyone, there was no true loyalty, and toxicity always rested right in the middle of us. They weren't my friends, but they were a way to keep my mind from being idle. At this point, I couldn't figure out which was worse, a raging psyche or a toxic group of messy girls.

At 9:00 on Saturday morning, we were all in Savannah's bright red car, listening to some music that I had never heard and speeding down the highway towards some mountain that Savannah frequented. When we arrived, we all stood at the bottom of the mountain and looked up. I wasn't sure if Savannah thought we were all training to be Olympian climbers, but, nevertheless, we all took off to the top. We talked and laughed while we made our way through the elaborate trails.

When we made it to the top, I looked out and thought to myself that the hike was worth the pain because it was so beautiful up here. I wished that I could experience that amount of peace each and every day. At that moment, I couldn't hear Meira, I wasn't worried about what was to come, and I was as clear minded as I wanted to be.

After about 30 minutes of us sitting on the ground at the top of the mountain and admiring the view, we started to make our way back down. That was when I felt it. Even though hiking makes you hot, this was a different type of heat that came over me. It was a familiar heat. I told the girls that I would meet them at the bottom, and I chose to jog down the mountain as a way to keep this emergence from happening. When I made it to the bottom, I felt a sudden jerk and it felt as if someone turned me back around on my heels to face the mountain. I wasn't sure why I was now staring at this mountain, but I was just stuck there, and I was looking up.

I saw the girls coming down the mountain and laughing, but I still couldn't move to walk with them towards the car. Raina saw me standing there and said, "Girl, I am hungry and thirsty. Let's go." I couldn't do anything but stand there and look up. She even turned around to face the mound to see what I was looking at. When she couldn't see anything out of the ordinary, she said, "Y'all, I don't know what's wrong with Mya." She walked away as if she were annoyed. By that time, I had been standing like that for about ten minutes.

They all got in the car as if that was going to make me come running, but when I didn't come, Savannah walked up to me and shook me by the shoulders. Then she said, "Mya, this is ridiculous. Come on. We are hungry!" Still, as much as I wanted to move, I couldn't. I was being held in place by an invisible force. My neck was even starting to hurt because of how far up I was looking. Savannah got really close to my face and said, "I'm calling Josh." Josh was Savannah's significant other who was friends with Aaron. I wanted so badly to stop her because I didn't want Aaron to worry, but I had no way of stopping her.

Behind me, I heard, "Hey babe, are you with Aaron? Can you please put him on the phone?" Then a brief pause before she continued. "Hey Aaron, we decided to come to the mountain for a hike this morning and Mya is acting really weird. We're trying to leave, but she's staring straight up towards the mountain. She won't answer us or look at us. I don't know what to do. She has been standing there for 20 minutes … Okay … okay … bye." She then came back and said, "Aaron is on his way." She walked away and they all went and got in the car while they waited for him to arrive.

In between Savannah calling Aaron and Aaron arriving, I could hear Meira. She was telling me that we had to wait for Moses to come back down the mountain.

101

Was she serious?! I had read about when Moses would go up the mountain and talk with God, but this could not be real. I knew that Moses was not coming down that mountain, but she would not listen to me as I tried to explain this to her in our shared thoughts as a way to get her to release me. Since I couldn't convince her, I was stuck standing there.

Soon, I could hear Aaron's voice talking to the girls. He rushed up to me, shook me, and called my name. I couldn't move. Then, he picked me up and when he did that, it was as if all of my energy drained out of my body and I passed out.

I woke up in my home to the smell of food, a glass of water sitting in front of me, and Aaron right next to me. He saw me lift my head and said, "Relax," as he handed me the glass of water which I drank quickly because I was so thirsty. Then he asked, "You hungry?"

"Starving." My voice sounded like that of a toad as I answered him. He got up and grabbed the plate of food that he had prepared for me. All I could think about was how I didn't deserve this man and how it was time for me to come clean.

I ate the plate of food that he brought me and then I looked straight ahead and said, "I'm ready, Aaron. I am sorry that it has taken me so long. I planned to tell you today, anyways. I went for the walk to clear my mind so that I could be prepared to talk to you today, but I guess the opportunity presented itself in other ways."

He looked at me and said, "I am ready to listen." I shifted my body towards him and told him everything. I told him about Noelle's death, when I first met Meira, I explained those different weird events that occurred around him like the blood on the door and the jewelry that happened while we were in South Carolina, and then I explained what happened today.

When I was finished, he looked at me for a while and then he stared at the wall past me. I could see that he was thinking. The silence that lingered between us was thick and full of questions, but I knew that I had to allow it. This was expected.

He then looked back at me and said, "Thank you for trusting me enough to share this with me. I know this couldn't have been easy. First I need you to know that I still love you and I will not leave you because of this." He got quiet again. I needed him to say more, and he finally continued with, "Why have you not gone to counseling, Mya?"

"I guess this was just a battle between myself and Meira so I couldn't fight hard enough to make myself go. Overtime, she wore me out and now, things are pretty much the way she wants them to be with her having way more control over me than she ever had."

"I think you should go." This was all he said. I could tell that there was no other option for me at this point. I completely agreed with him at this point and I told him just that. Unfortunately, neither one of us knew that it would be too late for simple counseling. I had enraged

Meira by telling this secret and she was ready to push me over the edge.

   After today, I realized that Aaron was who I needed in my life. The girls never spoke to me again even when I texted our group message to apologize for my actions. There was no need for me to continue to hold on to what God never meant for me to have.

Chapter 10

Present

I jumped up in a frenzy shouting, "Where is she? Where is she?!"

Dr. Horia was sitting on the edge of my bed, turned towards a nurse when I jumped up. She faced me and said, "Calm down, Mya. Whoever you are talking about is not here right now. You need to rest."

"Dr. Horia, I can't rest. I need to talk to you now."

"I need to talk to you as well, but I think we need to wait until you are completely rested."

"I am rested!" I almost screamed this due to my impatience with her. I need to talk to her about this girl and about what I found out.

"Okay. Okay. How about we meet in about an hour. How does that sound?"

"Okay." I wanted to talk to her right now, but I settled for an hour.

An hour later I was seated in my usual chair, as scatterbrained as I was when I first arrived here or maybe even more so because Meira was not supposed to be here. I had gotten used to her being gone.

"So, Mya, I will go ahead and tell you what the nurse told me and then you can tell me what actually happened when I finish." She began flipping through some notes that she was holding on her lap. "One of the nurses heard someone talking in a hallway where no residents are

105

supposed to be during that time of the day. She walked out of the breakroom where she was seated to see you walking all by yourself, but it looked as if you were being dragged. She said that you then stopped at the door as if you were waiting for someone else to open it and then you said "yes" and opened the door. She then saw you walk into the room and ask something like, "where is it?" She saw you once again appear to be dragged over to the window where it looked as if you became confused and then increasingly disoriented. You then turned as if someone was talking to you, you said a few more things, and then you passed out. She told me that she called for a few more nurses to come and help her get you back to your room and then she called me to tell me what she had witnessed. You did not sleep long before you woke up. Can you explain to me your side and who you were talking to?"

After hearing this, I felt a tinge of embarrassment and shame, but I knew that I needed to tell her exactly what had happened especially since I had agreed to be open with her. "Remember I told you about Ahlai Foe?" I started.

"Yes. I do."

When she told me that she remembered me telling her this information, I went on to explain everything from beginning to end. I told her about my first impression of Ahlai, the things I couldn't figure out about her that were bothering me, and then I told Dr Horia about the incident that just happened. I lastly went on to explain my last moments before I passed out. I told her, "When I turned to Ahlai, after being shocked at what I had just witnessed, she

106

called me stupid and told me something about telling me plenty of times not to put myself in this situation because they would try to take her away, but I didn't listen. I knew exactly who she was in that moment and I guess the weight of what I just realized overwhelmed me and caused me to collapse."

"That is quite the situation, Mya. I am sorry that this happened. Were you having any questioning thoughts about her before this incident?"

"I was. I thought so much about how familiar she looked and how familiar she sounded. I thought that some of the things she talked about were weird. She had a very odd obsession about the part of the Bible where the Israelites were in the wilderness. I found this weird because that was the era where Miera was stuck. She also would know things about me that I never shared with her, but she would convince me that I had told her previously when I would ask her how she knew certain things. I also found it off that she was always with me and it seemed as if she could hear all of my thoughts. The first time we went to approach that door, I was thinking about whether or not I could actually trust her and the weird feelings that I had around her and it seemed like she heard those thoughts and that stopped her in her tracks."

"This is all quite a lot, Mya, but I would like to provide you with a little bit of insight. This is not to frighten you but to inform you about what may be taking place." She paused briefly as she flipped through some pieces of paper. "I would like to let you know that, after my investigation, it has been confirmed that we have never had an Ahlai Foe here in any capacity. After hearing about all of this from you and from the nurse, it is very apparent what has taken place here. Ahlai does not exist. The person that you have been forming a relationship with is someone in your head. The nurse did not see or hear another person with you and the other personnel have never heard that name before. It appears that when I left, Meira made a reappearance. This is normal especially because we had not gotten too far into your treatment. I would like to reevaluate your diagnoses to make sure that we treat every disorder that seems to be present. In the next session, I will be providing you with more information about this. Are you okay with this?"

I took a deep breath and said, "Honestly, I am so tired of this. I thought I was progressing, but now I feel like I am back at stage one with this stuff. I want this all to be over, so I guess I have no choice but to be okay with it."

"I am so sorry that this is happening, but we will get through it. This is a process."

"Thank you, Dr. Horia." I said in a defeated tone because I was over it.

A couple of days later, I was sitting right back in the chair where I spoke with Dr. Horia about my roller coaster of a life. Usually, we have a session once a week, but my condition was considered urgent, so she wanted to get back with me as soon as possible.

"So, here we are again, and I think that we should just jump right in." Dr Horia said, smiling gently.

"Agreed," was all I could manage to say before she began rambling through more papers that looked like the first packet I received when I was first diagnosed with Dissociative Identity Disorder.

"Okay. Oftentimes, Dissociative Identity Disorder can be confused or may appear to be another psychotic disorder, like schizophrenia. I wanted to reevaluate to make sure that we could continue forward with your treatment plan for DID. The good news is that we can. It has been reported of other individuals with DID that they experienced some sort of visual hallucination which is what you experienced when you were in that room. This is simply related to posttraumatic and dissociative factors which both have to do with the diagnosis that I have already given you. To sum up, we will continue with the same treatment plan we originally spoke of since what you recently experienced is a symptom of your original diagnosis. Does this make sense?"

I sat quietly for a moment and then I asked, "Will this happen again?"

She must have been anticipating this question because she said, "We will work diligently to make sure that you are building the necessary coping skills, strong mental foundations, and support systems to prevent this from happening again. We are also in the process of hiring another therapist so that we can make sure that you and other residents of this hospital are being taken care of and seen on a regular basis."

"I guess that and the fact that I don't have more than one diagnosis makes me feel better. When will we begin my treatment process?"

"As soon as possible. You will be having more homework and more sessions so please be prepared for that."

"I'm ready," I said immediately because I knew that I could not go through another one of these episodes. This had to end.

Dr Horia handed me the papers that she had shuffled through and said, "These are for you. There is nothing here for you to sign, but I wanted you to have all of the information on your disorder so that you can be completely aware of what is taking place and what could happen."

Afterward, the session went on a little bit longer before we wrapped up. It appeared that the glasses that I was wearing provided me with nothing but an illusion, but I am confident that my new pair will reveal a world that I haven't seen in a while: a world of complete healing, true love, and wholeness.

1 ½ months ago

Graduation day was one of the most exciting and saddest days of my life. I was excited because I was finally done with this educational journey and had opportunities waiting on me. I was sad because Noelle couldn't be here with me. As I walked across that stage, nothing else mattered except for the fact that I had successfully executed this, not only for myself, but for Noelle. I graduated at the top of my class despite what had been going on. The service was very nice. We had an amazing speaker, we had thousands of friends and families cheering for us as we walked across the stage, and we had a huge class dinner planned for later that night as a last celebration.

Aaron had also graduated with me which was like the cherry on top of the cake. We had made many plans, and this was one of them. He had ended up taking a few extra credits his last two semesters to make sure that he would graduate with me. We wanted to stay on track for our plans together and I was ready to move forward with my life and into a new season. In addition, I had been staying with Aaron, in his second bedroom, because my lease was up and I didn't want to start another one when I knew that we both had plans to move away together soon. Even though we were closer than we had ever been, a couple of weeks before graduation, Aaron, seemed a bit secretive and distant. I was too focused to question what he was up to, but I made mental notes to ask him about his behavior later.

The day before graduation, I got a manicure and a pedicure and got my makeup professionally done before graduation. I knew I looked amazing and Aaron couldn't help but tell me so over and over. Even though Aaron was still acting weird before the graduation dinner, he treated me like a queen. He continued to rain down compliments as we got all dressed up for our black-tie themed class dinner. I had on a fitted, long, black dress, covered in glitter, with a sweetheart neckline, and a long spilt up the right thigh with some black heels. Aaron had on an all-black tuxedo with black shoes. When we stepped outside to leave, he had a Bentley waiting for us with a driver. I was shocked because we both graduated so I couldn't understand why it seemed like he was only celebrating my accomplishments. I almost felt guilty because I didn't even think to do anything special for him.

When we made it to the dinner, there was a red carpet for us to walk down and take pictures. When we got inside of the building, we were instructed to find our names on the table and have a seat. The entire space was extremely elegant. There were black, white, and gold with hints of red decor everywhere. More and more people started to trickle in and everyone was mingling until someone got on the microphone and told us that the evening was about to begin.

They started off by announcing that dinner would be served first and then we would move forward with the program. After a prayer was said, servers began walking around and putting plates on the table with food that smelled delicious. As soon as everyone had eaten, there were a few people that came up to talk to us and then they announced that there would be a slideshow of memories and then dancing.

The slide show started and everyone was laughing while some were crying at the memories. I was so into the slide show that I didn't even realize that Aaron had disappeared. I noticed that the slides of Aaron and I kept popping up back-to-back and I couldn't understand why. After about the fourth picture, everyone stood up and turned towards me as the pictures kept moving forward. One of the servers walked up to me, took my hand, and led me to an opening where the tables were split on either side. I was very confused, but I went along with it anyway. When I looked up at the other end of the opening, I saw Aaron looking back at me and then the music shifted from happy music to romantic music. Aaron had a microphone in his hand, and he began walking towards me.

Once he reached me, he said, "Mya, I know I have been acting weird and now, I can finally tell you why. First, I want to let you know that I am so grateful for you and that I appreciate you more than you know. You and I have had quite the relationship and most people would not have made it through, but we did, and we are closer than we have ever been.

"When I first walked up to you in class and basically demanded that you be my accountability partner, God told me then that you would be my wife. I was not about to compromise that, and I was not going to stop until you became just that. Finally, after much prayer and fasting, God has told me to ask you if you would do me the honor of becoming my wife." By that time, he was directly in front of me and had gotten down on one knee and said, "So, will you?"

I was crying at his first mention of the word "wife." I was crying because this was all so beautiful. I was crying because I no longer had to wonder why he was acting differently around me and whether or not it was me. Most importantly, I was crying because, despite me telling him about all of the issues that I had been dealing and was still struggling with, he still wanted to spend the rest of his life with me. I couldn't even open my mouth to say "yes" so I nodded my head and fell towards him to give him a big hug. He hugged me back for a brief moment, then he stood up, took my left hand, and slid a beautiful diamond ring on my ring finger. He moved back in for another embrace while our classmates stood all around us cheering. It was an unbelievable moment.

The rest of the night was full of laughing, dancing, and conversations until it was finally time to part ways with our classmates and go home. During the ride home, I was wrapped up in a trance thinking about how incredible this night had been, but there was a disgusting thought that I tried to keep pushing down and that I knew didn't belong to me. When I could no longer push the thought down, I had no choice but to listen to it and it was the voice of my nagging counterpart telling me that I didn't deserve this, and that Aaron was going to ruin my life while she had been here for me all of this time. She kept saying so many different things, but what I specifically remember is her

114

anger. I had never heard her that angry before and it let me know that something bad was about to happen.

When we made it home, I told Aaron that I was going to take a shower. I went to the guest bedroom, took my sleeping clothes out, and laid them on my bed. Then I walked across the hall to the bathroom. I started the shower so that it could warm up while I took the time to clean all of the makeup off of my face.

I took out some wipes, wet them slightly with warm water, and started wiping when I felt a wave of heat hit me like I had never felt before. I tried to keep wiping through the overwhelming amount of heat, but when I looked back up, my face looked very different and sinister. My head was lowered, but my eyes were staring up at the reflection in front of me.

I could feel my hands lowering slowly and I dropped the wipes and stood there for about a minute continuing to stare at my alarming reflection. My makeup was now smeared with half of my face still made up and the other half partially cleansed. I realized that I was staring at half of my face and half of Meira's face. A conniving smile spread across my face and made my lips curl at the ends. Then suddenly she punched the mirror in front of us with full force which caused it to shatter with a loud crash. I heard Aaron call my name and begin walking towards the bathroom when Meira picked up a large shard of glass. Fear was the last emotion that I could register before she swiftly and deeply pushed the sharp piece of glass into my wrist. I let out a blood-curdling scream as the

115

thick, red blood started flowing out of me at a fast pace. She lifted my other wrist and did the same.

I then heard Meira say, "I could have gone back to Egypt if I would have known that you weren't going to help me. You still chose everyone and everything else over me and now this will be the end for both of us." The last thing I heard was a crash through the door as Aaron rushed to me.

When I woke up, I was on a stretcher with medical wires and objects connected to me. I also noticed that my wrists were wrapped tightly. I tried to sit up but I was held down by the straps that were connected to the stretcher. I started to plead with the men that were taking me away.

Aaron must have told them that I was struggling with mental health issues. When they saw me, they came to the conclusion that I slit my wrists which is what made them decide to take me to the Goshen Psychiatric Hospital medical unit to get checked. Who knew that I would be spending more time than I bargained for at this place? And who knew that I would learn some of the greatest lessons of my life at this place?

Part 2:
Healing

Chapter 11

Calling my family and telling them what had taken place over the last few days was difficult but necessary. They believed that I was progressing just as I had believed so there were some defeated sighs and words of sadness. Even though I called them to tell them this less than positive news, they were all still very optimistic and encouraged me to keep going. I needed their support for this journey. Being so transparent and talking to my family and Aaron before the session gave me the strength to talk to Dr. Horia about some things that I had just discovered since the last time I spoke with her.

After getting comfortable in my normal seat in her office, she started with, "Today, I would like to take a moment to ask you if there is anything in particular that you would like to speak about as we move forward in your healing process. We'll allow you to lead today's conversation." Dr. Horia looked at me intently and patiently.

I was glad that she started the session this way because I did have a few things that I needed to share with her. "I do actually. To begin, I have a few things that I need to read to and show you. I was flipping through my journal just to look over my progress since I have been in this place and I discovered some excerpts that didn't necessarily come from me." I hesitated and then I started to open up my journal. I turned to the first page that I wanted to read and began reciting it word-for-word:

"This started out as a way of escape. After leaving Egypt, we remained in the wilderness for years. We were only supposed to be here for a little while, but because some of us chose to complain and rebel, we were punished by God. While all of the other people were stuck complaining,

I found Mya. This was my way out in part. I thought that this could go on forever and that I could eventually live out the rest of my miserable life through her. Why would she tell someone about this good thing we had going? Why would she put us in this predicament? She knew that these outsiders would attempt to break up our bond. In the beginning, things were smooth sailing because it was just the two of us.

When Aaron was around, I was put in the background. This didn't make me happy and I did what I could to maintain our bond. I was able to operate more through her when she and Aaron broke up. It was just the two of us again. My anger grew, though, when they got back together, and she told him everything. What is wrong with her? She acted like this was just so bad for her. What about for me? My anger led to us being in this hospital and, as I sit here writing in this hospital room, I have to figure out what to do next. How can I come back?"

I looked at her and she was just writing so I continued.

"I am weakening. I have to do something. Our thought processes are altered because of that stupid doctor. We don't need her help. We don't need anyone's help."

I stopped reading, and explained, "This statement was repeated over and over across three pages. It started off being written neatly and, by the end of the third page, it was written as if there were no longer any control over the writing utensil. The writing was large, sloppy, and barely legible."

Dr. Horia still said nothing and she kept her head down as she kept writing.

"The next thing she wrote must have happened when you went away for a little while," I said before I started reading again.

"That doctor is finally away. I am able to think, plan, and execute. I have decided that I will manifest into a girl named Ahlai and lure Mya back into my grasp. I have to be careful as to not set off any red flags. She has never seen me outside of herself so this shouldn't be too difficult. She won't recognize me. She can be so stupid sometimes.

Patience is the key to gaining her trust back. Patience is the key to reigning over my host. Patience is the key to having my way. I have my plan."

I paused to make sure that she was getting everything I was saying. Then I started reading again.

"Once again, it feels like I have lost. I feel defeated even though I am still here. I am still holding on. My plan on taking Mya into that room was supposed to be the

121

beginning of my reign, but they keep calling it a new start for her. I hate them…" I noticed she wrote "I hate them" over and over again.

"She wrote this statement so hard that there were holes in the paper," I told Dr. Horia the last part just to give her some context about Meira's physical and visible anger in that moment as she was writing in my journal.

Then I said, "She also drew a picture."

She looked up and said, "I would like to take a look."

The first and most obvious things were the two women in the drawing. They were the center of the photo. One of the women was on top of the head of the other woman. She looked like she was in a crouching position. She had strings attached to her fingers and they were connected to the head of the other woman as if she was a puppet. The other woman was looking down at a book, maybe a Bible, obliviously. In front of the two women, towards the left of the paper, there were a number of symbols. There were two swords, a golden calf, there were people kneeling in front of the calf, there was an altar, and there was a mountain with a single human standing at the top of it facing a bright, huge sun. Most importantly, there were many, many small x's raining down over everything except the two women.

We sat quietly as Dr. Horia examined this drawing and looked at the things that were written. She wrote a few more things down in her notes and then she looked up at me and said, "How does this make you feel?"

I had to sit in silence for a moment because, after all of that writing she had done, I thought that she had something more than that to say. "Well, first, I had no clue that this was written in my personal journal. It is a little creepy that I was sitting and writing these things, but it wasn't actually me. Second, her plan to take over my life is also scary because she seems so determined to prevail. I thought she was gone at one point, but she came back stronger than she ever had. She tricked me and it's hard for me to believe that I won't fall for something like this again or that she won't get even more creative with her antics. It also sucks because this will more-than-likely cause me to have trust issues when I meet and interact with new people."

"I can understand your fear, but I need you to know that because we have a better understanding of what is taking place, we know the diligence that we have to put forth. Our determination has to be greater than hers. Putting another therapist in place to make sure that there are no gaps in sessions will ensure that you get healed and gain control over your own life. I would like to speak about each aspect of what she wrote in your journal, though. I jotted down some notes as you were speaking. The first thing that I would like to point out is that now I understand why you had so much compassion for her in the beginning after hearing her explanation of her escape and why she was trying to escape. It is important that, no matter what takes place from this point forward, you remember that she is not real. This is an alternate persona that your mind has made up in an effort to cope with your previously traumatic experience."

She got quiet and I looked up at her with a thoughtful gaze. "Even though I learned some positive things from this experience, I believe that she hurt me much more than she helped. I almost ended my life because of an imbalance in my brain."

"I am glad you comprehend the seriousness of this. Next, from the second journal prompt that she wrote, we can see that therapy weakens her ability to control your actions. This should give you hope in knowing that we will be consistent in therapy, even when you are released, to make sure that this does not happen to you again."

I appreciate how she stops in between statements to make sure that I am still following. "Absolutely. I can see clearly how counseling is serving as a portion of my healing process."

"What do you mean by 'a portion'?" She looked as if she was expecting a specific answer.

"I mean that I will be meeting with Mike just as often as I meet with you to make sure that I am rebuilding my foundation on solid rock as opposed to shifting sand. Prayer and feeding myself with the Word of God is a big piece of this healing process as well."

She nodded in satisfaction. "Great. Moving forward. In the next piece she wrote, again, we can see how therapy impacts her strength. When I was not around, this was her opportunity to become strengthened and that is exactly what she did. Had I been here or had we had an

124

interim therapist working with you, she would have continued to weaken. Again, hope."

I simply shook my head at this reiteration of what was just stated.

"Lastly, we need to address the picture. What I am about to say is a little different than how I usually speak with you. It may sound more spiritual than clinical and it will also give you a little more insight into my personal feelings about your situation. I am only saying these things because it is something that I can clearly see and because I believe that we have built the relationship to be able to disclose some things that will positively contribute to your healing process. With that being said, I believe that we can see just how much this alternate persona wants to control you and how much she wants to separate you from God and all of those things of meaning represented in the Word of God. We both know that if we are not for God, then we are against Him. I think it is important that you draw closer to God than you ever have so that He will draw closer to you as His Word states. You have something intangible fighting against you which the Bible refers to as 'principalities.' I take this as a sign that you have something great coming up in your life that the enemy is attempting to fight off before you can ever make it to the point of reaching your personal promised land." This self-disclosure was much needed. It was necessary for me to hear from God in some way and He spoke through her about this current situation.

125

I had to open up my journal at that moment and write that last part down. "A sign that you have something great coming up in your life that the enemy is attempting to fight off before you can ever make it to the point of reaching your personal promised land." This statement helped me remember that my purpose is greater than what I was able to see. This was a perspective shift. I looked back up at her when I was done writing. She proceeded with, "Now, I do not believe that you will need counseling forever. I just believe that you will need it until you are able to retrieve those coping mechanisms that were shut down previously."

"Even though I am truly thankful for you, I definitely don't want to do this forever. I am ready to get through this process and become whole."

After a few more minutes of chatting and being given some homework assignments, I left Dr. Horia's office feeling great. To make things even better, I bumped into Mike as I was just about to make the turn to go into my room. He said, "Hey Mya! I was just coming down to speak with you about when our next meeting can be. Do you have a few minutes to chat?"

"Hey, Mike. Sure. I am free for the rest of the day. I just left Dr. Horia's office."

"Great. Are you hungry? Would you like to eat and talk?"

"Yep. Let's go."

We strolled to the cafeteria, grabbed our food, and made our way to an area towards the back. "So, how have

126

you been?" Mike asked as he picked up his water bottle and began twisting at the cap.

"I have been … better. I know that you heard about my minor setback, but I have received confirmation that everything will be great going forward. How have you been?"

"I am glad you're better. I have been great. Busy, but great. How has your spiritual journey been coming along?"

"I've come to realize just how much God has revealed to me through my personal situation and through the words of yourself and Dr. Horia. I hope that I can one day share my testimony. It's profound as I reflect on where I was to where I am now. I know that I have to start reading my Bible again and praying even more, now. Dr. Horia brought to my attention that I am under attack because of what God has in my future."

"That's good. I think that is so true. I am glad that you are realizing these things. Though, I would like to present you with an opportunity to share your testimony once you are in an even better place mentally." He looked up at me and I was anxious for him to tell me. I didn't say anything, and he said, "I have been able to observe your journey since the time you walked into this hospital and it has been profound. I have never met someone so resilient even when they feel defeated. I can see the light of God shining through you even when you don't know it's there. So, in these next few weeks of you being here, I would like for you to prepare a speech."

127

This was an amazing opportunity and it made me think that maybe this was a part of what the enemy was trying to keep me from. "About what? Where will I be speaking?" I asked.

"I would like for you to write out your testimony or anything that you think will impact the lives of others. I will be working with you each week and praying for you. I have a friend who's a Pastor of a very large church and he is having a mental health week. He tasked me with finding a speaker and you were the one person that came to mind. The last event will be a praise and worship session and they want someone to come and speak so they can celebrate with you and so that you can provide others with the hope that you have."

"Wow. That sounds like a great opportunity. I couldn't even say no if I wanted to because I just spoke about how I would like to share my testimony one day. I would, though, like to pray about it."

"Of course. I expected that. I am excited to work with you on this. God is going to do great work through you, Mya."

We talked a little bit more about this, decided that we would meet again next week, and then we left the cafeteria going in two separate ways. When I made it back to my room, I chose to start reading a book that I checked out of the library before Ahlai made her appearance a couple of weeks ago. Pleased with how this day went, I was able to peacefully read until I fell into a restful slumber.

Chapter 12

"Today, I want to spend some time talking about your spirituality. As you've mentioned previously, you have a history of being in the church and you have also had experiences since you have been here. I would like to remind you that this is a spiritually based mental health facility and so spirituality and faith is important here. Let's start with a few questions." Dr. Horia looks up for my approval and I nod.

"Did you grow up in church?"

"I did. As I continued to grow up and grow in my relationship with God, I decided to make the choice to continue attending church."

"What made you want to go to church?"

"I was driven by the need to have a relationship with God and the need to gain more knowledge about God and His character. Noelle also kept me encouraged during those times when I just didn't feel like going. Unfortunately, when Noelle died, it was difficult for me to continue on my spiritual journey because it had morphed into something that we did together. Church was where we grew and where our foundation was built ... or so I thought. I think my relationship with God was basically made through my relationship with Noelle."

"What makes you say that?"

"If I had a relationship with God and Noelle separately, I don't believe that I would have strayed so far

129

when she passed. Also, I think my faith was based on the good that God could do instead of Him in general. I was interested in His hand and not in His heart. My life went so well up until the point that Noelle died. When she was gone, it was hard for me to maintain my faith. I honestly didn't begin to realize this until after I came here."

"Did you ever try to go back?"

I sighed. "I did, actually. It didn't turn out so well."

"Well, first, what made you want to try again?"

"Hmm. I can't say that I wanted to try again, but Aaron and I had a conversation about it. He had asked me to go several times, but I ended up telling him that I just wasn't ready. The night of one of our later discussions, I had an interesting dream. Which, in a way, made me feel like I was forced to go to church with Aaron."

"How did that go for you?"

"It went completely wrong. It ended with me running out of the church after seeing the people around me turn into something I knew they weren't."

"Interesting. You mentioned a dream that you had. Would you like to tell me about it? Do you remember it?

"I remember it vividly." I proceeded to tell her about every detail of the dream that I had some years earlier.

After a pause so that she could finish writing down everything I said, Dr. Horia looked back up at me and said, "Mya, have you ever heard of Gestalt therapy?"

130

"Yes. I have. I am not a fan of it. I would prefer Person-Centered or Reality Therapy." I giggled.

She also laughed and then said, "I understand that, but I would like to actually try Gestalt Therapy today as a way to talk about the different parts of your dream and how they may have impacted you. The parts of that dream may reveal some things that we have yet to think about as a team. Make sense?"

"Yes, ma'am." I hesitated because I wasn't sure where this was going.

"Great. There are a few different aspects of your dream that I would like for us to analyze together in order to get a better meaning of the entire dream. Oftentimes, as Gestalt Therapists believe, the parts of the sum are greater than the total sum. In other words, analysis of the different aspects of your dream will give a more in-depth understanding of the whole meaning of your dream. The parts of your dream that I would like to analyze are the porch scene between you and Noelle, your changing face, the mirror, Meira and the other chanting figures, the things that were said directly to you, the red hue, Aaron and Noelle, and the church scene. So, first, close your eyes. Think about when you and Noelle were sitting on the porch in your dream. What feelings or thoughts come to you?"

I closed my eyes and thought for a moment before I said, "It … it feels comfortable. There was a feeling of familiarity. When she asked me what was wrong with my face, everything changed and I felt an automatic sense of

131

dread as if I knew that this wasn't just a common allergic reaction or something."

"Okay, tell me what you feel when you look in the mirror and see your face."

"Fear. I feel fear. I also feel something familiar, though, because I had already seen that alternate face on my body in real life. The face of Meira is now familiar to me."

"How does her face on your body impact you?"

I thought for a second. "Even though I can only see her face, I know that much more comes with her. She has control over my whole body which is how she's able to chant at me in the mirror using my mouth."

"Let's discuss the chant. What is happening there?"

"She is telling me to turn away and disobey over and over. This refers to when the Israelites were constantly turning their backs on God while they were in the wilderness. Then she tells me that we won't make it to Canaan anyway which refers to the land that God promised the Israelites and how many of them didn't make it to the Promised land due to disobedience. I know that she means this literally in her world, but in my world, it takes on a different meaning."

"Tell me what you think it means. Go with it."

"Umm…from what I have come to learn, she is not a good force in my life. She wants to make sure that my distance is maintained from God. She wants me to get it in

132

my head that there is no true success or any form of winning in this life. She is my enemy."

"What do you think those people chanting with her represent? Why don't they have faces?"

"I think that ... hmm ... I think that they represent the force of the enemy and his range of impact - the amount of influence that we underestimate the enemy having. The reason that they are faceless is because an identity of the force doesn't really matter when you are under attack as long as they can get you and keep you in their realm." I realize that I am beginning to like this type of therapy because it is making me see this dream much deeper than what it appeared to be on the surface.

"Wow. Okay. What about that red color in the bathroom? What does red represent to you?"

"I believe that it represents blood. It can either be the blood that can save me or the blood that is a result of death. It can represent evil or good. I think that the red hue was, at one point, there to let me know that I was under attack by the enemy and then it's meaning changed to let me know that I was being saved from the grasps of the enemy."

"Interesting, Mya. Okay. What about the chaos that was taking place?"

I had to think about his question a little longer. "I believe that it represents the fight that is going on within me. I know there is a fight for my soul. The evil forces are making noise to distract me while God is simply trying to

133

get my attention and pierce through the noise of the others."

"So, tell me about the period of silence that came next."

As I sat with my eyes closed, I could feel the sensation that came over me when everything came to an immediate halt. "I feel a sense of calmness. There is a sense of peace. It almost also feels like some sort of breakthrough."

"Breakthrough from what do you think?"

"A breakthrough from the chaos that was taking place at that moment. Maybe the dream represented what I needed to do to make a breakthrough occur and silence the chaos that was taking place in my head."

"So, then you found yourself looking in the mirror again to see both Aaron and Noelle looking back at you? Explain this."

"Yes, they were both there. They were whispering and telling me to cross over the Jordan River. I believe that God often speaks to us in a whisper and I think he was telling me, through two of the most important people in my life, to simply cross over into goodness and to stop allowing whatever was going on in my head to take control over me … wow…" As I said this, a revelation occurred.

"Great observation. Then you chose to open that door in your dream?"

"I did. The door led to the church where Noelle's funeral took place. That part is sort of difficult to think about … I … umm … believe that I was being reminded that, one, life is short and, two, I was being invited back into the arms of Christ. I also needed to realize that Noelle's funeral was the moment that my life changed forever." When I said those words and with my eyes still closed, tears began to roll down my face. I was now feeling the weight that Noelle's death had on me mentally and physically. I was so ready for that weight to be lifted and, in return, I knew that I needed the light and easy yoke of Christ. I could no longer hold back. I put my hands in my face and sobbed. I was partially crying out of sadness, but I was also crying because I knew that this was the heaviness leaving my body. Dr. Horia simply sat quietly as I continued to cry. I guess I underestimated the effects of Gestalt Therapy.

Finally, with my face a total mess and a weakness in my body, I boldly sat back up and looked at Dr. Horia. She looked back at me with an expression of success then she asked me, "How do you feel?"

I nodded my head and told her that I felt "different, but in a good way." Those were the only words that I could use to describe how I felt in that moment.

"Because our main goal was to talk about your spirituality, on a scale of one-to-ten, how is your relationship with God with one being that there is no relationship and ten being amazing?"

I thought for a second and then I said, "Probably about a five. Before Noelle's death, I was probably at a seven. I am definitely better than I was before I came here and after Noelle's death because I was probably at about a

135

three. Being here is allowing me to go through a strengthening process that I would not have gone through otherwise. Also, Mike has been a great pillar in this journey."

"What steps would you be willing to take to get from a five to a six by next week?"

"I've started reading a book about spiritual healing and restoration that I picked up from the library, I'll begin reading the Bible again, writing out my prayers daily, and my weekly meetings with Mike will be important."

"Those sound like great steps and I am willing to assist you in any way I can to help you achieve your goals."

After she said a few more things about the session, she gave me homework to journal about or draw a representation of those important parts from today so I wouldn't forget the lessons and things that were discussed. She also asked me to draw or write about any more dreams that I may have during the upcoming week. Lastly, she asked me to contact my family and invite them to next week's counseling session. I agreed to all of these tasks.

At that moment, I realized that Dr. Horia had cleaned my glasses thoroughly and provided me with a clarity that I had not had in years. I was so grateful.

When I left my session, I decided to take a trip to the art room to draw the picture that was already forming in my mind. I went to the far, left side of the room where the paper was located, grabbed some markers, and found a seat in the middle of the large room.

I first started out by drawing a thick, red line, horizontally, in the middle of the paper. I then drew what looked like the back of a person standing in front of a mirror that reflected her face. Behind the face in the mirror, there were many smaller faces with large mouths covering the majority of their heads. There also appeared to be chips and missing pieces in the glass of the mirror and the standing girl appeared to be slumped over and weak. There was also a toilet and a shower in the corner to signify that the dream took place in the bathroom. To the right, there was a door and what looked like lines coming from the door to resemble noise because Noelle was banging on the door in the dream.

The second part of the drawing, below the thick, red line, showed the back of the girl walking towards a preacher standing on an altar. The preacher had his hands outstretched towards her. Around her were many pews and many people in the pews. I was standing up straight and it looked as if I was about to take a step right into a small body of water that was in between the preacher and I. This represented the Jordan River that was mentioned in my dream. To finish off the drawing, I added some colors along with what looked like bright yellow light shining from the top corner of the bottom drawing to represent God's light that was now shining upon me.

When I finished completely, I walked to my room while admiring what I had drawn. I took a shower and then I grabbed my journal to do some writing and planning. I wrote out my dream wedding. It had been so long since I had actually taken the time to write about my wedding. It gave me so much hope to think about being out of here and in my own home with my soon-to-be husband. I wrote about this until I grew sleepy, wrote out a prayer, and then I fell into a deep and peaceful sleep.

Chapter 13

I was both excited and anxious about this session with my family. As I got dressed, I thought about the different scenarios that could take place. Would they be talkative? Would they be silent? Would they be sad?

When I made it to the door, I could hear the chattering and laughing voices of my loved ones on the other side. I removed the barrier between myself and them excitedly and they all jumped to their feet to greet me and hug me. I then took a seat right beside Aaron who immediately grabbed my hand in a grasp which lasted the duration of the session.

Dr. Horia started once everyone got seated and comfortable. "I would first like to thank you all for being here today. It is always amazing when the family is willing to offer support and help in this process. Mya, your family and I got a brief moment to speak about what today would entail. This will be not only a vulnerable time for you, Mya, but for them as well. We are going to go around the room and each person will talk about why they are here besides the fact that we are all here to support Mya. Who would like to go first?"

It was quiet for a second before Aaron said, "I guess I'll go first." He looked nervous. "I'm here because I experienced mental health illness and its impact on a family unit firsthand. My mother had schizophrenia. When she had me, her parents were no longer around, she had two siblings that lived in two different states, and she never married my father. Basically, she didn't have anyone around that she trusted enough to be open about. Also, as she was growing up, mental illnesses were considered a taboo subject and she never wanted to be called 'crazy.' I came to learn that because, when I was in high school, we had an incident at the grocery store and a man called her crazy. She showed him crazy that day." He chuckled and then his face turned serious. I held his hand a little tighter.

"I would hear her talking and arguing with someone in her head all of the time. She was extremely paranoid. She often talked about someone watching us and she wouldn't allow anyone to come over to the house out of fear that they were one of the 'them' watching us." He displayed air quotes with his fingers when he said the word "them."

"Eventually, all of our windows were boarded up, she would rarely leave the house, she would check all of my clothes when I would come home from school for wires, and she would always talk in a whisper and make me do the same." He took a deep breath, and I could see a tear forming in the corner of his eye. "A few years ago, I came home from school and I found her passed out in the middle of our living room floor. She would take pills that would make her slightly sluggish and the bottles of those pills were lined up near her right arm along with two empty water bottles as if she just took all of the pills and tossed them to the side. I wanted to run up to her, I wanted to scream, I wanted to panic, but I couldn't. It's sad to say

140

that I almost felt a sense of relief because I knew that she would be happier away from this earth.

"After that, I went to go live with a friend of mine for a while until I went off to college. I even went to a counselor a few times to make sure that I was okay. My friend and his family were big on going to church, so I was going with them faithfully. It was then that I had an experience with God that changed me. I spoke with God so much about my mother and what I could have done differently. He didn't tell me those things in that moment, but, when I met you, He instructed me to stick by you no matter what. He also told me to make sure you knew that you were never alone in your trials which was something I couldn't do for my mother at the time." He was crying and so was everyone else in the room. I hugged him tightly until he was crying no more.

Dr. Horia waited a minute and then she said, "Thank you so much for sharing, Aaron. Your testimony is remarkable. Who would like to go next in telling us why you chose to come here today?" She looked around the room as she said this.

My mother then said, "Well, Mya, I wrote you a letter letting you know about my past with my mother and siblings along with my own personal bout of multiple personality disorder. I came here not only to support you, but to finally speak, out loud, about my story and how I overcame. I won't go back into details, but I will let you know that I understand how it is to live with someone that attempts to control your life, who does things without your

141

permission, and who can't be seen or heard by anyone but yourself. I know how it feels to not want anyone to know for fear of being judged or abandoned by those close to you. Just like Aaron, I had an encounter with God and through your situation, He revealed to me that I must be the support that I never had from my mother. He let me know that I must provide you with the love and care that my mother was incapable of giving. I came here to let you know that you are an inspiration to all of us because, even though it took you a while to get to this hospital, you were receptive and resilient once you got here and are allowing God to glow through you and strengthen you like never before."

"Thank you, Mom. I am also so proud of you." I reached my hand towards her and she grabs it and squeezes slightly.

"Thank you so much for sharing." Dr. Horia nodded toward my mother and then said, "The floor is open to whoever wants to share next."

My aunt jumped right in and said, "I guess it's my turn. As you know, I grew up in the same household as your mother. She shared the letter with me that she gave you so you're aware that things got physical when my mother hit me with a cast iron skillet. My journey turned out different, though. Instead of developing a mental illness at that time, I ran to someone that turned out to have one. My husband's dependency on drugs took a toll on my health and I found myself dealing with physical problems due to stress, anxiety, and depression. I chose to go to counseling which absolutely helped, but I am still coping with these issues each and every day." She took a breath and then she continued, "I am not only here to support you, but to gain lessons through you. I have seen the work that God is doing, and I am here to allow your light to make my life brighter."

I reached out and touched her hand. She did not cry hard, but she did allow us to see her emotions through delicate tears. It was finally my father's turn to speak and, when he realized it, he took a deep breath and said, "I honestly never had an experience, knowingly, with mental illness before I met your mother. Even though, at the time, it seemed like something negative to be exposed to, it was actually very eye opening and it gave me the space to view mental health issues as something common like physical ailments as opposed to something taboo or something stigmatized. If I'd never been exposed when it happened, I would have continued through life with a partial shade over my perspective and I wouldn't have been so understanding when it came to you, Mya. I am grateful for your mother in many ways, but this one had to be one of the most important lessons that she could have taught me; how to be a pillar and not a stumbling block in the life of someone dealing with psychological issues. I am here for you because I believe that the first time, with your mother, was the lesson, but this time is the test."

"Thank you, Dad. I believe that you are passing with an A+." I smiled at him and then I looked at Dr. Horia for what was to come.

143

"Thank you all for sharing and being vulnerable." Dr. Horia said. "I would now like to know how you all perceive this situation. Tell me your perspective in one or two sentences. This will help me get an understanding of your thought processes and how all of you can grow and be conducive to the healing process of Mya." She pointed at Aaron and said, "The floor is yours again."

"Well, I perceive this situation as scary, unfortunate, and unfair, but I also see it as an opportunity to learn."

"Great." Dr. Horia said and nodded towards my mother.

"I see this as slightly familiar and an opportunity to place blame upon myself because I did not speak up earlier about my past." My mother held her head down as if she wanted to cry.

"Interesting. Okay," She next pointed to Aunt Camilla.

"This is an opportunity for all of us to come together as a family and stand in unity. Sometimes it takes negative situations to bring people together."

"Awesome. And lastly," She motioned towards my dad.

"This is also familiar to me, but I look at this as a way to apply what I learned from my wife all those years ago." My dad smiled and held my mother's hand.

"Great! It sounds like most of you have a positive perspective. I would like to point out that this situation is no one's fault. No one knew that a traumatic event would cause these circumstances. It is now necessary that we

144

focus on what to do from this point forward and not dwell on what could have been done. The next and last question is, "What can you do, moving forward, to make sure that you are emotionally available to continue helping Mya now and for when she gets out? Anyone can answer first."

My mother started on a more positive note. "I don't know if everyone would agree with this, but I believe that having these types of sessions as a group would be beneficial. We are all able to communicate in a peaceful setting with no distractions and we're able to fully listen to one another. I think that this would also help Mya because we would be able to learn more about ourselves and those traits that could trigger certain things within her and other people."

My father chimed in. "I never really considered counseling. So many people associate therapy with inadequacy or a form of weakness. I never wanted to be seen that way. I needed to maintain my appearance of strength. I guess it was a pride thing that should never have existed in the first place. I agree with you, honey, that these counseling sessions as a unit are beneficial. I also want to add that I am willing to go to counseling on my own to make sure that I am comprehending and depositing everything in my mind in a way that will not harm me in the long run. I need to do this to maintain my strength. This is a form of strength."

"I am so proud of you." My mother said this to my dad as she interlaced her fingers with his and gave his arm a hug.

After a beat, my aunt let them know that she was also willing to participate in these types of sessions and then she added, "Mya, you and I have a close relationship. We have always been able to talk about everything even when you couldn't talk to your parents in the moment. I believe that I can help you by being more intentional with building on the relationship that we already have, speaking to you more often, actively listening to you, and even listening to my inner self and my own feelings."

Everyone nodded after Aunt Camilla stopped talking and then Aaron spoke up with a big smile and said, "Now that I am about to be a part of the family, I will be attending those sessions as well." He looked so excited and everyone giggled a little. He always knows how to lighten the mood.

"We are just excited as you are about that, Son." My father said to Aaron with a big smile.

Aaron continued, "I will also go to counseling on my own to make sure that I have processed my past correctly and to make sure that I create the capacity to stand up against whatever may come. We took a break in our relationship and I will never do that again. I believe that can be assured if I go to counseling and learn how to truly cope in the midst of difficult circumstances. You are about to be stuck with me for life, so I want to make sure that I am healthy as well." He smiled at me as he said the last part and I smiled back.

"This session has gone so well. I am hearing support, love, gratitude, understanding, and willingness.

146

With that being said, I have homework for all of you." She got up, went behind her desk, and pulled out four journals. Each of them was different. "These are for you. I gave Mya one previously and now I would like to give you all one. These are for you to write in every day. Write your feelings, your thoughts, songs, ideas, anything. You can also draw if that is what you want to do. I believe that feelings and thoughts are more manageable, and ideas are more achievable when you have them written down in front of you."

She handed one to each of them and received 'thank yous' from them. "Today's session has been amazing. I believe that we all received so much insight about where to go from this point and how we can all help in this healing process."

I chimed in at that moment and said, "Yes, I am so grateful that I have such a great support system. I love each and every one of you." I stood up and they stood up as well. I hugged them close, then we chatted for a few more minutes before they left.

"Well, Mya. That was amazing. Wouldn't you agree?" Dr. Horia said this to me as soon as the door shut behind my family. She invited me to sit down so that we could have a brief one-on-one session.

"I absolutely agree. I am truly blessed to have them."

"Is there anything that you would like to talk to me about?"

"Actually, there is. I had a dream." I took out my journal and started to read what I had written when I woke up early this morning.

"I was sitting in a theatre production. I don't remember what it was about or who was even there. The play was still going on and, when I got up to leave, everyone abruptly turned their attention and blank faces to watch me as I walked outside. I looked at my surroundings when I got outside and noticed that across the parking lot, there was a strip mall with different stores. All of the other doors were glass to match the surrounding windows. One door, though, stood out because it was wider than the others and it was a metallic, black color. I chose to walk through it even though I had no clue about what would be waiting for me on the other side. When I opened the door and took a step inside, I saw dying plants everywhere, old yard appliances, old junk yard items, and I saw a girl sitting at a table with connected benches, alone. She invited me to sit next to her by simply motioning her hand not saying a word, and, when I did, we started playing a simple card game.

As we continued to play, I noticed that her movements matched mine exactly. It was as if she knew what I was thinking. A few minutes later, there was a shuffle behind me, and the girl jumped up from her chair. On her face was a look of pure terror. She grabbed my hand and dragged me from the table and out of the door that I had just entered not too long ago. When I glanced back to see what had made that noise, it was a walking color in the shape of a very large person. The red figure was now blocking the doorway. We kept running until we got to my car, which was parked in the parking lot between the theatre and the shopping strip.

When we got in my car, she didn't have to say anything to me, but, somehow, I knew exactly where she wanted me to go. We went to a restaurant. The outside of the restaurant was the same color as the door from earlier and the inside appearance of the establishment seemed very peaceful and quiet. There were food, drinks, chairs, tables, and people. When I looked a little closer, I realized that everyone was sitting alone. Everyone also looked as if they were deep in conversation with someone that wasn't there. I chose to mind my business and get my meal.

Once I was seated at the table, I looked over only to realize that I had travelled there alone, and, like everyone else, was now about to engage in deep conversation with someone who only I thought was there.

I woke up. I didn't wake up afraid or anything. I woke up and immediately thought about the meaning of what I had just experienced in my mind.

Symbols that needed to be discussed with Dr. Horia and maybe Mike: theatre, parking lot in between the theatre and shopping strip, the black door, the girl, mirroring movements, the red figure, knowing where to go without her telling me, restaurant scene."

I got quiet and looked up at her from my journal to let her know that I was done reading.

"What a dream. Have you taken the time to think about what the parts of the dream represent?"

"I have. Though I would like your perspective on what you believe it means."

"Sure. Let's discuss it. The first thing that you mentioned was the theatre. When I think of the theatre, I think about masks and actors. What comes to your mind?

"The same thing, but I wasn't sure how that applied to my situation."

"Well, for the longest, you wore a symbolic mask so that others wouldn't know what was going in your mind. I believe that you played the part of what normal was supposed to look like." She said the word normal and made air quotes with her fingers. "It seems to me that this aspect of your dream is a flashback to who you were and what you were doing to maintain the positive regard of others."

I was writing as she was talking. This was great. "I didn't think of it in that way. It makes complete sense."

"The next thing you mentioned was the parking lot between these two buildings."

"I immediately thought about being in an in-between space."

"Exactly. That space in between where we were and where we are going is so important. I believe that it can be referred to as the wilderness. I believe that this wilderness relates to you and your particular situation in a couple of different ways. The in-between for you could represent your transition from hiding to healing and

150

embracing what has occurred within you as a revelation of some sort."

I was, once again, writing everything down quickly. This was too good to miss and I knew that I wanted to reflect on all of this once the session was over. I nodded and then said, "Now I believe that the black door was a representation of me entering a space of the unknown and a space that is different because the door was different than those around it."

"Great observation. I can't disagree with that one. The walk across that parking lot transitioned you. The next part was the girl and the connection that she had with you. I think this one is pretty obvious. Wouldn't you agree?"

"I do. I know that this represents my alternate persona. I found it interesting, though, that she appeared after I started my transition."

"Well, she did appear while you were here. She was a part of you for so long, so it is possible that she still exists within you which is why we are so diligent and consistent in your treatment."

"Okay. Now the red figure. The color red showed up in my last dream. I think it represents me running from both the enemy and God."

"Why are you running from God?"

"Well, it was because I blamed Him for a long time for what happened to Noelle. I just couldn't grasp the fact that He would do something this dramatic for a testimony. Now, I understand that this type of content makes the most impactful testimony. I understand that I am here to help

151

and provide the wisdom to others that God has provided me through my circumstances."

"Wow. It is amazing to witness what is taking place within you. I agree with you. I would also like to add that I don't believe that running from the enemy is the best thing to do either. You have the tools you need to fight against whatever is holding you back or pulling you down"

I smiled at her and then said, "The last part was the restaurant scene. This one was slightly creepy to me, but I believe that it represents multiple things. I have gotten so used to Meira that when she is completely gone, I may feel a sense of loneliness. It could represent how I saw myself as an insane person who is always talking to themselves. It could also be a representation of this hospital; a place where many people are being stripped of their mental illness and being kept in isolation for a certain amount of time."

"You said a mouthful. You have become very observant and self-aware. Overall, I think that this was a very positive dream and interpretation. I would like for you to continue writing and focusing on your progress. I also need for you to understand that it's okay to not be perfect during this journey. You will have days where you feel defeated. It is important that you keep pushing forward and looking towards the goal."

"Thank you, Dr. Horia. I can feel the change happening within me and nothing will make me go back or stop my progress. Today's session was amazing."

She said a few more things and then I got up out of my seat and started walking towards the door. Today was another successful day and another step towards recovery. I soon learned that the decision to stay committed to this recovery was even more important.

Chapter 14

"I was standing outside of a carnival. It was nighttime so the lights on all of the rides and the booths were illuminating the sky. From the outside of the fair, it was a beautiful scene. I began to walk closer towards the carnival from a parking lot where there were no cars. As I got closer, I could see there were so many people, though there were no cars. I also noticed that even though I could hear laughing, I couldn't see anyone's face at first because everyone was moving so fast. Why were they speed walking everywhere?

Suddenly, everyone started to slow down, and I could see faces. The first face that I caught a glimpse looked oddly familiar. As I continued to look at the faces of the others, I realized that everyone's face was the exact same whether they were dressed like a woman or a man. I soon realized that I was looking at the face of Ahlai. I felt panic beginning to rise in me, but before it could even happen, I was pushed to the entrance of a small hut-looking tent with 'Future' handwritten on a piece of cardboard. I decided to walk in to escape the confusion that was going on outside.

Inside was a woman with the face of Dr. Horia, but her body was almost shriveled up which made her look much older. When she saw me, she stared at me for a second too long and then she invited me to sit down on an old, red chair in front of her with a motion of her hand.

When I sat down, the cushion of the chair was noticeable and memorable because there was a slight prickly sensation almost like a dull cactus underneath the red cushion. After I got past the feeling of the seat, I looked up and the lady was just staring at me like she had before, but her hands were shuffling a stack of cards and laying them on the table in front of us. She finally took her eyes off of me and looked down at the cards which made my eyes follow her gaze.

When I looked at the cards, I noticed that they were alternating between solid black and solid white with ten cards in all. I looked back up at her and she was, once again, just looking at me. I started to very awkward, so I got up slowly and walked back outside to the chaos of the carnival. As soon as I stepped outside of the tent, I realized that everyone was exhibiting different emotions: anger, rage, sadness, happiness, confusion, fear, anxiousness, peace, frustration, and more. I took off running to the parking lot where I was before and ended up in the same position, looking back at the carnival from the outside, just like in the beginning of the dream.

Interpretation: These dreams are getting more and more vivid. Dr. Horia taught me the strategies, though, to be able to interpret them on my own and understand what could possibly be taking place as my subconscious attempts to make sense of the external world. After thinking and praying about the meaning of this dream for a while, I think I have come up with a meaning. Overall, I think that this dream represents the different emotions and

155

struggles that I will have on my journey. I think that it also represents me choosing to look at the beauty of the circumstances. My perspective.

When I closed my journal, I sat for a minute to try and gather myself and my emotions, but I could only hear the ugly thoughts in my mind.

"This is so exhausting."

"I have been dealing with this for this long, I don't see why I can't just keep on dealing with it."

"People are going to judge me for being in a mental hospital for this long."

"I won't be hirable. They will find out that I was in a mental hospital and determine that I'm unfit and incapable."

"I will always be at a deficit."

This was my morning. In addition to these incessant thoughts, there was confusion because I was unable to tell if these were my thoughts or if they are the thoughts of my alternate identity. It had been a while since I had experienced defeating thoughts of this magnitude, but I assumed that this was all a part of the process.

I pushed myself to get ready and reminded myself that this was a day that I would be meeting with Mike who was always able to take what seemed like something negative and turn it into a lesson and a positive.

"Hi Mya, how's it going today?" Mike said as soon as I showed up in the doorway.

"It's … going, I guess."

156

"Just going?"

"I guess I should just start out by saying that I feel extremely defeated today." I had to be honest from the start so he could understand and read my demeanor.

"Well at least you're acknowledging those feelings. Most people try to hide behind a façade of being okay. What can God do with feelings you try to keep away from Him, right?"

I huffed and said, "I'm trying to do better with that. I know that I have to acknowledge everything that is within me whether it is good or bad."

"Sounds like you are doing a good job with that. Your transformation is taking place. If it were easy, would it really be worth it?"

"Hmm. I guess you're right. Thanks for that. It feels good to know that I am moving in the right direction and being honest with myself."

He allowed for a moment of silence and then asked, "What do you think is making you feel defeated?" Mike was sitting on the floor and rifling through a box of books. I actually liked the informal meetings that we had. It seemed more inviting to me; more like a conversation than an interrogation.

"I am just having a lot of thoughts that are bringing me down. You know? Thoughts that are discouraging."

"Our thoughts can be a powerful thing. The Word tells us that what we think in our hearts, we are. Those thoughts have the power to transform us. However, those thoughts can be an attack from the enemy which I take as

157

a compliment. Anything that is happening in the natural represents something happening in the supernatural. Anytime the enemy sees positive change towards God, He has to counteract that with one of his fiery darts. I don't think it would make any sense if he attacked people who were already working for him whether they know it or not. If I were the enemy, I would attack people that work to tear down my kingdom and build up the Kingdom of God. We just have to make sure that we are able to decipher the voice of God from every other voice so we can limit confusion."

All I could do was look at this man. He spoke these words out of his mouth like they were a second language all while searching through some old books like it was nothing. He just blew my mind with his words and acted like nothing happened. "I don't think I have anything else to say." I slightly giggled. "With what you just stated, my mind, body, and soul just completed a 360-degree turnaround. I think I'm good now." He thought that was funny. I laughed with him, but I was serious.

"I am glad I could help. Found it!" He yelled this out as he lifted up a book out of the pile that he had created. I jumped a little at his exclamation. "I have looked through five boxes full of books for this one, small, book." He pointed at the book after he stood back on his feet. "This book has gotten me through some hard times, and I have been hearing God telling me to pass it on and I made the decision to pass it on to you."

He handed me this old brown book with one word across the front of it: "Redemption." I looked at it for a second. I couldn't really find the words to say, but I knew that this book would help me transform into the woman, mental health issues or not, that I was supposed to be. "I don't even know what to say but thank you."

"Thank me after you read it. Now, let's talk about the event." He clapped his hands together like he was so excited. "I have a little more clarity on what this will look like for you. For the most part, it will be fun but also informational. We want you to interact and partake in the activities if you desire. Regarding your actual speech, they would like for you to talk for only a short time. They don't want to put too much pressure on you. Have you at least started to work on what you would want to say?"

"Kind of. I have thought about the elements that I would like to touch on."

"And what are those?"

"I would be honest in speaking about how I got to the hospital first. I would talk about what I learned through my experience, the importance of having your own relationship with God, making sure that you talk about what you may be going through with family, friends, or a mental health professional, and how God used my situation for purposes greater than I could ever imagine."

He nodded his head with a look of satisfaction on his face before he said, "It sounds like this will be one powerful speech. I also want to encourage you to ask God what He wants you to say."

159

"Definitely. I don't think I would be able to do this without him."

"I am glad you know that."

There was not much that needed to be said at this meeting. Mike, once again, allowed God to effortlessly speak through him which set me straight in a short amount of time.

I went to the cafeteria, ate, and then I went to the art room to read. I knew that it would be quiet there and they also have comfortable chairs in the back of the room. I decided that I would read most of the book since it was a small one. As I began reading, I started to take notes in my journal.

- *Redemption, Vindication, Saving, Reclamation, Repossession*
- *What in my life needs redeeming?*
- *After the saving comes the lessons and the healing process.*
- *Healing, Alleviate, Relieve, Ease, Help*
- *The healing process should come with a perspective shift. During my process, how has my perspective changed?*
- *It's not about what ailments you have, whether they are physical or mental. It's about how you handle what you have.*
- *It's not about the trials and tribulations that come up against you, but about how you handle them and yourself during them and how you proceed through*

160

*your wilderness stage. Will you complain? Will you
fall into a depression while thinking about how life
would be if you didn't have whatever you think is
holding you back? Will you choose to use your
impairment as your weapon of mass education,
information, and wisdom? Will you actually step
outside of yourself and selflessly help and interact with
those that may be in the same boat as you?*

- *How would you live your life if your ailment never went
away?*
- *Don't allow your lesson to be a complete loss due to
your negative perspective and thoughts.*
- *Your thoughts can have a major impact on perspective,
behavior, and action.*
- *Hold your thoughts captive and make them obedient to
Christ (2 Corinthians 10:5). How? Weigh your
thoughts against the Word of God. Are my thoughts
true, noble, just, pure, lovely, of good report,
praiseworthy? (Philippians 4:8)*
- *Invite God in, allow myself to be saved by Him, allow
him to transform me through the renewing of my mind
(Romans 12:2), allow my perspective to shift from me
to what God needs me to do, use my experience to
touch other people.*

Even though I believed that I knew what perspective was,
I was now able to understand what perspective actually
means and how to take true control of it.

Chapter 15

"I was riding on a black and white horse up to a very large church. The horse was perfectly striped. Outside of the church and standing in a straight line was Noelle, my mother, my father, my aunt, Mike, Dr. Horia, and Mrs. Lamire, the teacher of the class where Aaron and I met. I was on the horse and then I wasn't. I was standing still and then I was walking into the doors of the church following behind the line of people who were just a moment ago standing still and watching me approach.

As I was walking down the aisle, Aaron was dressed in all white. When I looked down, I had an all-black dress on, black shoes, and black jewelry.

When I reached Aaron and he took my hands, a warm feeling came over me and everything that I had on turned to a beautiful, pure, glittery white. When the change happened, everyone in the church stood up to their feet. While everyone was standing, the pastor was talking, but I could not hear him. Aaron and I exchanged rings and we kissed. We celebrated as we walked out of the building and approached the now all-white horse that was waiting for us."

I only had enough time to write down the dream before it was time for me to get up, get dressed, and start my day. I decided that I would think in depth about the dream later. I was looking forward to seeing Aaron at today's counseling session, however, I was not sure if I was looking forward to today's topic of conversation. I sighed as I gathered myself.

An hour later, I was sitting next to Aaron in front of Dr. Horia speaking about something that I hadn't really spoken much about out loud or even to myself. "In that moment, it was unbearable. I never really understood true heartbreak until that day. My tears almost burned as they ran down my face. I literally felt a part of me die even though I couldn't get my mind to catch up with the reality of what was taking place. If I could have, that night when I ran around the house looking to see if she had escaped, I would have run lap after lap until I saw her again. I would have run myself to death if I would have known the amount of pain that was going to follow." I put my head in my hands and began to cry. Since the day that Noelle was buried, I had been consumed with the issue that was evolving in my mind. I never found another time to sit and think about the actual situation that caused my grief and sent me on this horrible journey. "It's been years, and the pain still exists, like the night that the house went up in flames." I said this as best as I could through sobs.

When I was able to pick my head back up, Dr. Horia was looking at me and Aaron was holding his head down looking at his hands. "I think about what it must have felt like to helplessly be burned alive. I believe, sometimes, that it should have been me and not her. I think about the smell that I smelled earlier that day and how I should have taken the time to figure out where it was coming from instead of ignoring it. She would have done a much better

163

job at life and coping with the aftermath of this tragedy than I did. She was so amazing, and she didn't deserve this. I question what she did to die so terribly."

Dr. Horia sat quietly for a few more minutes because my tears wouldn't let up. Aaron just sat quietly rubbing my back. Eventually, Dr. Horia spoke up. Her voice somehow helped alleviate my tears. "Thank you for being so open and vulnerable with us. Mya, I need you to understand that you need to be here just as much as she did. We never know why things happen to good people, but we do know that everything happens for a reason. It seems to me that so much has happened since her death. Let's talk about that."

I took a moment to breathe and then I said, "Well, on one hand, I developed a mental health illness that evolved to a point that almost killed me. I almost lost the love of my life. I was unable to develop any meaningful friendships. To top it off, I am now in a mental health hospital. On the other hand, my faith is stronger, my perspective has shifted, and God's presence is the strongest that it has ever been in my life. My issues have brought my family closer together and helped them realize the things that they may need to change. I have also graduated from school with two degrees - one for her and one for me. And finally, I've been presented with an opportunity to share my testimony and am now able to see that the positives of my situation greatly outweigh the negative." As I was naming the positive aspects, my heart began to smile because I was so proud of the changes that

164

had occurred in me in what seemed like such a short period of time. I looked over at Aaron and he was also smiling.

"It's great that you are able to identify those things that have changed in your life and that your perspective has shifted so greatly. That is important in your journey. I do want to be honest with you, Mya." I felt a sudden surge of anxiety because I was not sure what would come out of her mouth next. "Because Dissociative Identity Disorder does not yet have a cure, you will have to take extra care of yourself, more than the typical person, to make sure that you maintain healthy coping mechanisms and to make sure that you don't retreat back into the grasp of your alternate persona." She stopped talking for a moment and just looked at us. "I would like to know your honest thoughts about how you feel about this."

Both Aaron and I sat quietly for a few more seconds before I spoke up and said, "Well, the good news is that I remembered you telling me that DID had no cure when I first made it to this hospital. The negative part is that I am almost at the end of my journey and I have not thought much about how I would maintain outside of this controlled environment. I guess it's time for me to start thinking. What about you, Aaron?"

"When I asked you to marry me, I asked for all of you. I am willing to do what it takes to make sure that you maintain your mental health. I will even do coping mechanisms with you to maintain my own mental health." When I heard him say these words, I thought about how blessed I was to have such an amazing man in my life.

"This is so good to hear. It provides me with great relief that you two are so accepting of this process and support one another so strongly. Now that we all have that understanding, I would like to talk about coping mechanisms. The main thing to remember is self-care. This is one of the most important parts about maintaining good overall health. Self-care could be going on a walk, doing deep breathing exercises, listening to music, or even taking a second to sit in the car before walking into the house. We often associate self-care with some grand activity like travel or massages and, even though those still can be considered self-care, minor acts are also important." She handed us a paper that had a list of easy self-care activities that could be accomplished under five minutes.

She continued, "Other coping mechanisms could include talking to someone or asking for help, lowering your expectations about a person or a situation, meditating and praying, and exercising, or even laughing." She handed us another piece of paper that listed coping skills that could be easily developed.

"Now, when it comes to Dissociative Identity Disorder, it is important that you maintain a relationship with a counselor wherever you go. This does not mean that you have to see them every week or even every day, but it is important that you have a professional to make sure that you are still on a great path. They can also identify any changes within your behavior even if you don't." Again, she handed us a third piece of paper with this information

166

and different counselors that she would recommend in the state of Virginia.

This was quite a bit of information to take it, but I guess I appreciated the numerous amounts of coping skills and self-care activities. There was no excuse for Meira to make another appearance. I also appreciated the papers that she gave us so that I could be reminded of what I needed to do. "Thank you, Dr. Horia, for all of this. I guess it's important for me to really start thinking about this. I do want to live a healthy life once I leave this place." Aaron didn't say anything. He just nodded in agreement.

"You're very welcome. I want you to be healthy as well. Until you find out where you will be moving, though, I would suggest you continue to work with me. You would no longer come to this hospital but to my office. Many clients from here continue to work with me until they find another option if they choose to find another option. This is something I want you to think about." She paused briefly to make sure that I understood. I nodded. "For homework, I would also like for you to think about some self-care activities that you already do and then think about some that you are willing to incorporate. You both have your journal so please utilize them." She smiled at us.

She then lightened the conversation and asked us about the wedding planning and moving. I had not been planning as much as I should have since we wanted to get married soon after I was released so that we could move away. "Well, I know that we don't want anything big, we want to make sure that our family and friends are in attendance, and I want a beautiful dress. That's about as far as I have gotten." I giggled a little. "We don't want to spend too much time thinking about this small step. We would rather spend our time making sure that we have a lasting and healthy marriage."

"That's a great way to think about it. The wedding is the easy part. The marriage is where the real work begins."

"We have definitely heard that multiple times and we take it seriously. I am ready to get this thing started." Aaron said this as he looked at me and gave me a kiss on the cheek. This guy still gave me butterflies.

"Okay. I just wanted to do a quick check on that." Dr. Horia said as she got up from her chair to put some things on her desk. We talked for a few more minutes before it was time for Aaron and I to go meet with Mike.

We left Dr. Horia's office and went straight to Mike's office. He seemed so excited to talk with us which made us excited to talk to him.

"I am so glad that you two were willing to meet with me. I know that this can be a difficult journey especially when you are also trying to plan a wedding and prepare yourself to move away."

"Yes, it definitely is, but the planning keeps my mind from drifting to the negative and keeps me focused on the important things," I said.

"That's great. I would first like to ask you two if there is anything that you would like to talk with me

168

about." He sat back in his chair and waited for one of us to speak up.

"Actually, there is." I told him. "I realized, today, that I blame myself for the death of Noelle and that I feel guilty. It is also hard for me to come to terms with the fact that I am still living, but my friend is no longer here, and that God had something to do with this."

He sat for a minute quietly with a look on his face that signified he was thinking. "Yes, Mya, that is a difficult one. A few different things come to my mind. The first thing is to remind you that we will never know God's thinking when it comes to the things that happen in our life unless He makes them known to us because His ways are higher than our ways and so is His thinking. Another thing is that whether or not God had something to do with the death of Noelle, He works all things together for the good of those that love Him and those who are called according to His purpose. I truly believe that you love him and that your purpose is in Him. Would you agree?

"Absolutely!" I said this without hesitation.

"Something else that's coming to me is the fact that even if the death of Noelle and the attack on your mental health was the work of the enemy, God will take what the enemy meant for evil and turn it for good."

At this point, I had to take out my journal and start writing to make sure that I recorded everything from God that came out of his mouth. After I got done writing that, I looked back up at him like I was taking notes for a test.

He then asked, "Do you remember the story of Job?" We both nodded. "Do you remember how God allowed the enemy to attack Job just to prove Job's faithfulness to God?" Once again, we gave Mike a nod to let him know that we were following. "Well, have you ever considered that when it comes to your life? Have you ever thought of all of these events as trials to prove your faithfulness to God and a setup to be able to show God's goodness? I want you to understand that God is instructing you to rejoice because your reward is great in Heaven. Rejoice in this fiery trial so that, when His glory is revealed, you may experience exceeding joy."

"You said a powerful mouthful, Mike." Aaron said this almost in awe.

"I never know what the Holy Spirit will say through me." He laughed slightly and then said, "One more thing. I think that this whole season could have also been a call back to Christ or a way for Him to get your attention about something. Sometimes, God will use the situations, good or bad, of other people to get our attention. Before we move forward, I would like for you two to think about what God has drawn your attention to in this time and whether or not you have actually given Him your attention."

Mike could barely finish his words before we were writing down our thoughts. I think I knew that God was trying to get my attention this whole time, but this conversation solidified that idea. I wrote in my journal:

*God drew my attention to his character, to forming
my own relationship with him as opposed to just having a
close relationship with others that have the relationship
with Him, the importance of perspective, understanding
that I am not alone and that I cannot operate as if I am
alone, the pertinence of making sure I maintain
connections with the people that He put in my life, and His
love that He reveals to me through His Word, His Spirit,
and through His people.*

Soon after we took that minute to write, we started
talking about me and Aaron's relationship. We needed to
make sure that we were prepared to take on marriage. Mike
started off by asking questions about our sex life, kids,
career goals, finances, household duties, things that bother
each of us, and more. He also told us to write down why
we want to get married to each other in three sentences.
We took another moment to do this and I wrote:

*I want to get married to Aaron because he is
someone who never gave up on me even when he wanted
to. He listens to God which is the most important thing,
and he listens to me. I could not imagine anyone else as
my husband and I could not imagine my life without him
as my husband.*

I read mine out loud first which put a big smile on
his face and then he read his. "I will marry Mya because
this is God's plan for my life. I have been blessed with a
life altering and life lightening woman and I will not pass
up the opportunity to marry her regardless of any fears that

I may have. I have never been surer of another person in my life." It was my turn to have the big smile on my face.

"Aaron, you mentioned fear." Mike inquired.

"Umm. Yes. Sometimes I do feel fear. I think its fear of the unknown or maybe even fear of not being the support that Mya needs. I know that these are thoughts that are not of God so I remind myself that faith will always replace any worry that I have."

"That's a great way to think, Aaron. If we operated out of fear, we would all be stagnant in our growth, in our journey, and in life."

"Thanks for that reminder, Mike." Aaron replied.

Mike nodded and then said, "After hearing all of the information that you have given me and your reasons to marry one another, I don't think I have been more excited for a couple. You two have been through so much and it would make me so happy to see two wonderful people in a happy marriage. Do you two have all of your plans mapped out? I know that can be a lot."

"We're getting it together. We wanted to find a venue that doesn't cost a lot because we only want to have a small event and we'll be moving right after." Aaron was doing most of the planning, so I was glad that he spoke up.

"Hmm. How would you feel if I made a call to check on a location for you?"

"That would be great! Please let us know about that."

"I will. Also, after talking to the two of you and coming to understand the bond that you two have, I would like to ask, Mya, how would you feel about Aaron coming to speak at the event with you for the mental health week that my friend's church is having?

"What?! I would love that! We could speak about how this journey has been for the both of us and how it helped us grow."

"That would be perfect because many people believe that mental illnesses run people off and have the potential to ruin relationships, but you two can prove that that's not true all of the time. You all can share your unique story and inspire others that may be going through similar issues. Aaron, what do you think?"

"I'm always willing to inspire others and if Mya is excited for me to do this with her, I'm excited as well. I would just like to know the details as soon as possible."

Mike handed Aaron a flyer and let him know that we would be speaking in front of a large crowd on the last day of the event. He also let us know that he wanted us to participate in the entire week if we could. "I am really looking forward to this and I believe that it will be worth it for you two as well." Mike said this with a small smirk.

After the session with Mike, Aaron and I talked in the hallway for a while before he had to head back home. It was so great having him here today and experiencing his love for me. Even though I had to talk about how I felt when it came to Noelle's death and even though there were tears, I felt peace, joy, and gratefulness because of the support that I had to help me heal and because of the many revelations that were taking place.

I went back to my room and decided to finish up the interpretation of the dream that I had written down earlier.

Black and white. White is the absence of color while black is the presence of all color. White is pure. Black is tainted and has been introduced to many things. In my dream, Aaron represented white and I represented black. When I touched Aaron, my dress and shoes turned white and glittery. I believe that this represents the emotions between Aaron and I. Before meeting him, my emotions were more negative than they were positive. He brought a spark (glitter) to my life that transformed me. He is God-sent.

Chapter 16

"Noelle and I were sitting on the couch. I couldn't hear what she was saying because the dream was inaudible, but I knew that we were laughing and that we were happy. It looked like the scene from the night that this nightmare first began. We watched television until we both fell asleep. Everything still appeared the same as that night except it looked like we were watching a bright red screen with nothing else on it. I watched myself wake up and walk to the bedroom, leaving Noelle asleep on the couch and falling asleep in my own bed.

My view then changed to an overhead one as if I were looking into a doll house without a roof. It was like an out-of-body experience. A little while later, I saw a small light glimmering behind the stove in our kitchen. It grew quickly and then it caught onto the towels that were hanging on the oven handle. I watched it spread throughout the kitchen and I could still see us sleeping. The fire made its way to the living room where it caught onto the rug, the chair, and then the couch where Noelle was still sleeping.

I looked back at myself and I was now standing up in the middle of the room facing the door, but it appeared that I was still sleeping. I looked back at Noelle and she was now engulfed in the fire. She was slightly floating above the couch and still peacefully sleeping. I also saw another figure standing over her. It was so unreal. I *immediately thought about Shadrach, Meshach, and Abednego when they were thrown into the furnace in the Bible. When I looked back at myself, I was now laying on the grass outside of the home while the house was completely in flames.*

I then woke up from the dream. I had never seen such beautiful and graceful fires in my life. I feel a sense of peace as I am writing this. God revealed to me that Noelle is in a place of peace with Him that she would have never reached had she remained on Earth with us. She is protected. He also let me know that every ugly situation has a beautiful side. This goes right back to perspective. Thank you, God."

I closed my journal and leapt off my bed. I danced around my room as I continued to pack the remainder of my things. Today was my last day in this place. Today was the start of my new life as a healing and healed woman of God. My parents and Aaron told me that they would be there to pick me up around noon and it was right at 11:00 in the morning.

I heard a knock on my door, and it was Mike and Dr. Horia. The looks on their faces showed me just how proud of me they really were. I had developed a deep relationship with these two that I planned on maintaining when I left here and even after Aaron and I moved away. "It looks like you're all set to go." Dr. Horia was the first one to say something.

"I am so ready." I said with excitement. "Even though I probably grew more here than I did in my entire life, it's absolutely time to go."

"Well, we just wanted to come by to let you know just how much a joy it has been having you here. Not only did you grow, you also pushed us to grow as well. You inspired us and reminded us of our purpose in doing what we do. This was an amazing experience for us and I hope it was for you." Mike's voice almost sounded like it was getting shaky as he said that last part. Dr. Horia nodded in agreement with him.

"I am so, eternally grateful for the two of you. I wouldn't trade this entire thing for anything. This was needed."

"We both wanted to give you something as a goodbye gift. You can open it when you get in the car or something." Dr. Horia stepped forward and handed me a small box wrapped in shiny red paper. Then, Mike handed me a note.

"Thank you so much." I gave them both a hug and then stepped back.

"We'll let you get back to it. Your family will be here soon. They will have all of your discharge papers at the front desk and that will also include my information for when you are ready to set your appointment with me in my office." Dr. Horia said.

"Yes, and you have my information so we can keep in touch about the upcoming event." Mike said.

"Yep. Thank you!" They turned and left.

177

I finished up my packing and, soon after, I was in the car with my parents and Aaron headed away from the hospital.

On the ride home we chatted for a while as they shared our plans for the night, and then we eventually turned the music up and relaxed for the rest of the ride. I took this as an opportunity to take out the box that Dr. Horia gave me. Inside was a silver, chain-link bracelet with a small tag on the front that said "Healed." It was so simple, but it was a reminder of my journey and transformation.

I pulled out the letter that Mike handed me next. I opened it and began to read.

"Mya, you have truly been a light to my life. It has been a pleasure knowing you and helping you and I am so grateful that I get to continue speaking with you and Aaron after you leave Goshen even if it is only briefly.

I wanted to provide you with a little bit of a gift/proposal. Remember when I told you that I would like to check on a location for you and Aaron to hold your wedding? Well, it turns out that they would love to host your wedding and, after hearing briefly about your story (I gave them a little insight because this is a center which is a part of the church that you and Aaron will be speaking), they told me that they wanted to do this for you with all expenses paid. This would include the building which holds about 100 people, a two-day building rental, the decorations, and a photographer and videographer.

178

I hope this will work for you. Because the mental health event is coming up, you two can let me know if you want to accept then. Looking forward to seeing the two of you soon!

Thank you again, Mya.

Mike

I immediately put my head in my hands and let out a sob. I was truly blessed to have people in my life that deeply cared about me. I startled everyone in the car with my random crying. They turned down the music and began questioning me. I couldn't dry my tears enough to speak so I handed the letter to Aaron who read it out loud.

After he was done reading, it looked like he wanted to cry. He said nothing because of his total disbelief. My mother screamed out, "This is amazing! I can't believe this!"

"Wow, just wow!" my dad said. He also seems to be in disbelief.

Aaron finally spoke up. "I researched the average cost of small weddings in America. $20,000 to $30,000. You mean to tell me that the cost of our wedding will end up going down to only a percentage?" He shook his head. "This is beyond amazing and I am beyond grateful." He grabbed me and hugged me. There was no doubt that we would be taking Mike up on this offer.

We finally made it home. When we walked in, there were balloons and Frenzie and Grace ran up to me in excitement. It felt so good to be so supported. I walked right up to my room where I set my things down. I wondered why my room looked so bare, but I just assumed that most of my things were still at Aaron's place.

I went back downstairs and asked Aaron where he would be staying for the night and he told me that he and my parents decided that it would be best for him to stay the night because we all had something important to do in the morning. I asked him to elaborate, but he just told me that we should go eat and that I would find out tomorrow.

After dinner, I chose to get some rest instead of staying up and writing in my journal since I knew tomorrow was going to be a long day. I was told to pick out some comfortable clothes, so I pulled out some yoga pants and a t-shirt. I took a shower, crawled in bed next to Grace, and drifted off to sleep.

The next morning, I woke up to the smell of coffee. I went ahead and put on the clothes that I had taken out the night before and then I went downstairs to greet everyone. They were all dressed as well, and it looked like they were just waiting on me. "Want coffee or breakfast before we leave?" My dad asked.

"I'll just take something that I can eat in the car."

"Okay. We have some granola bars in the pantry."

I walked over, grabbed one, and put it in my purse. They must have been up early because they were ready and waiting at the door.

We were soon seated in Aaron's car; Aaron and I in the front and my parents in the backseat. He warned me

180

that the drive would be a couple of hours so I could be prepared. I nodded and put on my seatbelt.

About an hour and a half later, Aaron turned to me and said, "I love you, Mya, and I hope you know that I will do whatever it takes to make sure that you are happy and whole. While you were in the hospital, I was offered a job as the director of health and wellness at a megachurch in Richmond, Virginia." This immediately caught my attention, and I drew in even closer to him. "I took the job because I knew that we had talked about moving there."

"Aaron, I am so happy for you! This is such great news. When will we be moving out here? Have you already started working?" I had so many questions.

"Thank you, my love. I started working and it has been amazing. The only downfall was that I didn't have a place to live out here so I would travel back and forth and rent hotel rooms for weeks at a time. This pushed me to look into some first home buyer options and Richmond had a lot to offer. I wanted you to be able to come home to our actual first home. Your parents and I did quite a bit of research and I think we found the perfect home for us, Grace, and possibly a future family."

"Is that why we're traveling right now?"

"Well." He pulled out a key from his pocket and handed it over to me. There was a tag attached to it that said, "Welcome to your new home from Reality Realty."

"Aaron, what is this?!"

"We will be pulling up in a minute."

I sat quietly and looked at the key. There was just no way that this man was this amazing. He had already done so much for me so I couldn't imagine him doing what I think he had done. There seemed to be no limits to what this man was willing to do for me.

I was fixated on the road especially when we took an exit and drove down into a neighborhood where the cozy, modern looking houses had about an acre of yard space. We finally stopped at a home on the corner of two streets. I looked at Aaron and all he did was nod at me. I undid my seatbelt, jumped out of the car, ran over to his side, and jumped into his arms. Aaron went through the process to buy us our first home. We were homeowners. I also hugged my parents because they helped him with this process.

I ran up to the front door and used the key that he had given me to open up the big, wooden door. The house was beautiful with an open floor plan. I moved quickly through each room of the house and admired every detail. I was also surprised by how beautifully the house was decorated. When I made it to the master bedroom, I realized that this was why my room at my parent's house looked so bare. This bedroom was so large with three doors connected to it. One was the bathroom, and then there were two closets. I opened up one closet and all of Aaron's clothes were in there. I opened up my closet to see most of my clothes, but there was a small desk in the corner of the closet with a sign over it that read "war room." I walked over to the desk which had books, two new journals, pens, highlighters, and the Bible on it. Aaron took the time to set up a place where I could spend time with God in solitude. There really was no end to the goodness of this man.

I walked back towards the front of my new home where Aaron and my parents were standing and waiting for me to complete my tour. "So, how do you like it?" Aaron asked.

"I absolutely love it! This is perfect. We have enough room for ourselves and for guests. You also gave me a war room. You are so amazing. Thank you so much!" I was beaming with excitement. This just couldn't be real. "We even have a yard for Gracie to run around."

"I am so glad you love it. I knew you would, though. Oh! I also want to show you something else." He grabbed my hand and walked me towards the back door. When he opened it, to the left and right under the windows was a garden. He explained that he had planted some flowers and that he'd also planted some vegetables. He said that he wanted to have a hobby on the side. I thought it was great. Until I found a job, I was so willing to tend to the garden.

"So, when will I officially be moving here? I know that we have the speaking engagement and our wedding."

"Right! The plan is that you will officially move here after the wedding. I will be here, for the most part, but you will be back at home. I will be back and forth. For most of the mental health week, I mentioned to your parents that they should go with you since I will be working here until the day that we have to speak."

"Okay! That sounds like a great plan to me." I took a second and just looked at him before I said, "Aaron, thank you so much. I am so blessed to have you in my life. I cannot wait to see what God has in store for our life together."

We walked back to the living room where my parents were and we talked about what was next. We decided that we would go view the surrounding areas, grab some lunch, go by the mall that was close to our home, and just do some sight-seeing to get acquainted with the area before we headed back to my parent's home. This was one of the best surprises ever. I couldn't even express my gratitude in words. When we made it back home, I made sure to write about this day in my journal so that the emotions and gratitude would never be forgotten.

The next day, when we were all awake, Aaron decided that he should go back to Richmond to prepare for work for tomorrow. My parents chose not to go to church, but they asked me if I wanted to go and visit Noelle's grave since I hadn't been since she was buried. I couldn't turn that down, so we got ready and drove to where she had rested for some years now. Even though it was something that was discussed while I was in the hospital, I guess I still felt some guilt because, when I walked up to her grave, the first thing I did was apologize to her for not being there for her like she was there for me.

That guilt can get so heavy so fast because I felt a weight pushing me down and in a matter of seconds, I was on the ground crying. I was letting every emotion flow out of me like a rushing river with no end. My parents stood back and allowed me to have this moment. When they believed that it was time to go, they approached me, picked me up off of the ground, and walked me back to the car. I had no clue that this visit would have this impact on me.

When we made it home, I went directly to my journal and began writing my personal psalm to express my emotions.

"Heavy like an elephant being pushed down by the hand of God

Culpable like the malicious murderer of thousands

Anguish and confusion like being mentally and physically attacked and controlled by a person who doesn't even exist.

Unable to forgive myself, unable to forget, unable to rise, unable to fall, I am fastened to the past and stagnant in my current.

I am simply existing and discontent in my present.

I am longing and rushing to escape my past.

I am running towards my future in an attempt to hurry it to be my present."

Something then shifted in me and this psalm took a turn. That overwhelming amount of sadness was snuffed out by a blanket of peace and joy.

"But that was the past.

185

Today, still with many flaws, Joy has replaced depression,
Peace has replaced worry and anxiety,
confidence has replaced insecurity,
selflessness has replaced self-indulgence,
focus has replaced a distracted mind
Instead of being completely destroyed, I am pieced back together by the Potter, having cracks that remind me of the journey which molded me into who I am today.
I am being watered on the inside and a garden of internal and eternal beauty is sprouting."

Chapter 17

Today marked the kickoff of the mental health week at the church where Aaron and I would be speaking. My mother was the one that decided to attend most events with me since my father and Aaron would be working. We did some research, found the full schedule of events on the church's website, and decided that we would go to all of the events except for day two.

Day one was all about relaxing the mind, body, and spirit. There were areas set up for yoga, meditation, mindfulness practices, and sound bathing. We chose to do thirty minutes of all four sessions. The sound bathing was something that I had never done before and was willing to do again. Everything was great, but the meditation and the mindfulness practices reminded us to remain present which was especially important for me. We felt very relaxed after this day.

Day two was dedicated to the kids which was why we made the decision not to attend. The children were going to learn about mental health and how to cope if they were experiencing mental health related issues. If I did have children, they would have been attending.

Day three was entitled "Trauma and Toxicity." There were different seminars and booths all focused on trauma and how not dealing with trauma in the proper manner was like poison to our minds. I learned that firsthand. One point that stuck with me was on a brochure at a trauma booth - that we should not have to deal with mental illnesses on our own and we should always seek support. Without my support, I don't think my transformation would have been as dramatic. They also spoke about how toxic relationships could have an impact on our mental health, how we need to seek God in the midst of seeking our support system, and how the belief that mental health illnesses were less serious than physical illness also fell into a toxic category.

Day four was particularly memorable because there was a sermon about taking our thoughts captive and the armor of God from a pastor who also had a background in the field of psychology. It was great to hear someone speak who understood the mental health aspect and who had knowledge about the Word of God. He was able to put these subjects together seamlessly which drew me in. I took my journal because I knew that there would be some things that I would need to remember. He even went so far as to talk about dopamine, serotonin, neurons, and the synaptic cleft in our brains and how each of the pieces could play a part in the development of mental health illnesses. He blew my mind with his knowledge and godly wisdom.

Day five was focused on physical activity and health. There was a run for mental health wellness where we could run, bike, jog, crawl, or whatever, an obstacle course for the kids, and healthy food trucks. We did the 5k walk and then went and got some baked fish street tacos with coleslaw on top which were so delicious. There was also music and dancing which made the day even more enjoyable. After the run, we ran into Mike who showed me where we would go for tomorrow's event and how we would enter the stage for the speech.

Day six was the big day and it was called "Destigmatized." Aaron came in the night before and we went over what we would say and how our speeches would mesh together. Today was the day to execute that plan.

We were backstage when we heard the speaker introduce me and invite me to come out. He handed me a microphone as I smiled and waved my hands at the large crowd of people as if I had all of the confidence in the world. I felt like I did because I was solely depending on God to speak through me. Aaron would come out a little later.

I started, "Good evening, everyone. Thank you so much for having me during this busy week." I took a moment while everyone got resituated after welcoming me in by standing and clapping.

"When we look at something, we tend to believe that what we see is true. We trust our eyes and ourselves enough to take what is in our field of vision for what it appears to be. That chair is a chair, right?" I pointed at the chair. "That screen is a screen, right?" I pointed at the big screen that was to the right of me. "Well, what if you could no longer trust your perspective? What if what you saw was not true or reality? This was a part of my mental health disorder. I was diagnosed with a disorder called Dissociative Identity Disorder or DID years after the onset

189

of the hallucinations. DID is a disorder that is usually described as one where a person develops one or more alternate identities."

I waited another second before I started again. "I wore rose-colored shades growing up with my best friend. The day that she died, those glasses fell and shattered on the cold, hard ground and, right after that, the ground fell from under me as well. My relationship with God was also compromised because I had built it with the person that was now gone. The alternate identity that had developed within me came as a result of the traumatic situation of losing Noelle to a house fire.

"My alternate persona was a young lady named Meira who was an Israelite in the Bible days and was in the wilderness with God, Moses, and the other Israelites. Because she was in search of an escape, she would sometimes operate through me and do things through me that I usually wouldn't do. Sometimes, I wouldn't even be aware of what had taken place. Because I believed that what I thought was going on would be considered too weird, I kept my illness to myself. This lack of talking about mental health issues is why it is referred to as a stigma. After a while, it had become too big of a monster for me to hide and I ended up having to tell my now fiancé who is here with me today. Aaron?"

He walked out just as confident as I had. The claps died down and he said, "Thank you all for having me."

"This is the person that reintroduced me to the importance of having a relationship with God and made me recognize the seriousness of communicating whether I wanted to or not. Aaron, how was it having to deal with someone you loved having mental illness?"

He turned to the crowd to answer my question. "Well, it was hard, and I could clearly see how relationships could fail due to mental illnesses. However, God took the time to work with me and provide me with daily reminders of why it was so important for me to stick by her side. We often tend to run when things get difficult, but, with God, the obstacles were more manageable. In addition, my mother committed suicide as a result of her mental health struggle, so I was determined to never let that happen again."

I nodded, and said, "When we talk about this, when we share our testimonies, when we avoid running away, and when we take the time to educate ourselves, then, and only then, is when mental health will become destigmatized."

"Absolutely. Coming to understand what resides in us and sharing those things with others helps us to embrace our God-given purpose." Aaron said as I nodded in agreement. "Being on the journey with Mya allowed me to recognize my calling to ministry and even those qualities that reside within me. What about you, Mya? What did your journey help you realize about your purpose or calling?"

"That it is so important that people understand that they are not alone. Someone has to be willing to share their testimony and bring glory to God without shame. This

191

journey taught me to do just that. For so long, I operated under the stigma and allowed my fear to stop me from getting the necessary help that I needed. I know that there are many people like me that couldn't bring themselves to communicate what was going on. My purpose is to share how God took a situation that appeared negative and turned it around for my good, to be a therapist, and to spread the Word of God through my testimony. It is also to help other people transform their perspectives and gain lessons instead of losses."

"I like how you mentioned lessons instead of losses," Aaron said. "That's a big one that people should attempt to grasp. When something as big as a mental disorder impacts one's life, it's so hard for people to have a positive perspective or see above the current circumstance. I believe that my lessons were to make sure that I am always listening to the voice of God, to never operate out of fear, and to fight for what I want in my life. What lessons did you receive from God, Mya?"

"That is so amazing, Aaron, and that's also a great question. I believe that I received so many lessons from God. God needed me to learn about who He is, His character, and how much He loves us. I needed to form my own relationship with Him instead of depending on others who had a relationship with Him. Even though my alternate identity was going through the wilderness, I was also experiencing my own wilderness when I was in the mental hospital. I needed to learn how to communicate and be open and honest with those people that God had put into

192

my life. Thinking that I was alone was an enemy to my growth.

"I also needed to shift my perspective and align my thoughts. I like to look at my situation as a sort of revelation. A revelation about who I was, who I depended on, who I trusted, God's grace, and God's unique way of communicating with each and every one of us. There were many, many lessons so I know that this isn't even half of them. Even though I am still dealing with my mental health issues, I feel happier than I ever have because I let go of pride, I got help, and I learned how to manage this."

"That's definitely a great start in attempting to explain just how God uses our circumstances and what we think is an ailment to bring others to Him and glorify His name." Aaron said.

We walked towards one another, grabbed hands, and then walked towards the front of the stage. "In closing, we would like to mention the reason why we agreed to come up here together. Making sure that you are not alone if you are going through something is important. God provided me with a life partner that was willing to go through anything with me. Mental illnesses do not ruin relationships when you have people around you that are God sent, it strengthens relationships. Together and united, we are able to destigmatize and normalize conversations around mental health."

Everyone stood to their feet in excitement as they clapped their hands, whistled, and whooed. We stepped back as the associate pastor who had introduced us stepped onto the stage and said, "Let's give it up for Mya and Aaron one more time." The crowd got even louder.

When they calmed down, the pastor said, "Mya, Aaron, on behalf of the church and the staff, we want to present you with a gift. We know that you all will be transitioning and getting married soon so we decided to present you all with a check to make your move a little less stressful." He smiled and handed us the check.

"Thank you so much!" Both of us responded simultaneously. Blessings were overflowing in our life and we were so grateful. This was our season of overflow and blessings.

We exited off of the stage where Mike met us. "Hey, you two! You were so insightful. Thank you so much for coming. I wanted to speak with you two about the letter. Let's go to a quiet area where we can talk. The lead pastor will also meet us there." We followed him to an office where the pastor was already waiting for us.

"Mya! Aaron! I'm Pastor Gerard. It's so great to have you here. I have heard so much about you. How did you two enjoy this week's events?"

"Everything was wonderful. We appreciate you for having us." I responded.

"So, Mike told me that he discussed our proposal with you. When Mike came to us with your situation, he only asked us to pray for you, but I would like to let you know that we were led to act and do this for the two of you. How do you two feel about this?"

"As soon as we read the letter, Pastor Gerard, we knew that we would humbly accept. We are in no position to deny any blessing and we knew that pride would be the only thing that would make us deny such an offer."

"This is such good news! Now, we can set up a meeting to discuss logistics because we do want everything to be to your liking. I need to run now to close out mental health week, but we will get together soon. It was great meeting the two of you and thank you again for coming." He rushed out of the room and darted to the right.

"Mike, thank you so much for all you have done for us."

"You two are very deserving and you have favor with God which is something that He gave us understanding about."

"That's good to know. Well, we don't want to hold you up any longer so would we need to set up the meeting now?"

"Yes. Aaron, you're working in Richmond so would a weekend be better for the two of you?"

"Yes. That would be best. Next weekend would work if you all have availability then." Aaron said.

"I think that would be great. If anything changes, we'll let you know."

"Sounds great. Thank you so much, Mike."

"No, thank you!"

We exited the office and then the building, meeting up with my parents before heading back to their house filled with feelings of success and gratification.

A week later, we were headed back to the church for the meeting. The first thing that the pastor and Mike did was show us the building where the wedding would be held. It was a nice, modern, and cozy building just right for the amount of people that we wanted at our wedding. It also had bathrooms and dressing rooms which was perfect.

After our tour was complete, we sat in four chairs and discussed who would be marrying us, decorations and colors which were gold and pink, rehearsals, rental time, what is and is not allowed on the property, and a few more things. Overall, this was going to be an easy process. We simply needed to take care of what we would be wearing and our reception. We had also previously decided on a staycation in our new home and that we would do a big vacation for our first anniversary, so we didn't have to worry about it at this time.

About an hour later, all our ideas were written down and we were leaving with no worries and complete trust in the people that God had placed in our lives. Beautiful simplicity is what I would call our approaching wedding and our life as one.

Chapter 18

One of the first things that Aaron and I did when I got out of the hospital was gather the necessary paperwork that we needed to obtain our marriage license since this would be a fast-paced process. When it came to the actual wedding, my mother, aunt, and I were quickly able to find a wedding dress last minute. It was white with a sweetheart neckline, fitted bodice, which flared out into a princess style dress with silver glitter. The dress was perfect for me. The morning of my wedding, my mother, aunt, and I went to get our nails, toes, hair, and makeup done. We were able to bond and laugh which helped alleviate some of the nervousness of the day.

Soon, I was in the dressing room of the building that Mike and the church had blessed us with. As I was sitting and looking in the mirror at myself, all I could think about was how fast this day had come and how joyful I was. This was the day that I would get to marry the man that changed my life in so many ways and that God blessed me with. I looked down at my journal where I had written my vows, read over them one more time, and ripped out the sheet of paper, folded it, and handed it to my Aunt Camilla who was my maid of honor. We took pictures, had conversations about marriage, and got in place for the ceremony to begin.

The time finally came for me to walk down the aisle with my father and meet Aaron at the end. With tears of joy rolling down my face, I took step after step towards my future leaving behind my past as I knew it. I looked up and saw tears flowing down Aaron's face as one of his college friends was standing by his side as his best man. When I reached him, he gave my father a hug, took my hands, and guided me up onto the altar where we went through the process of becoming one.

We listened to Pastor Gerard as he prayed over us, spoke to us, read Bible verses and then gave us instructions to read our vows. This part of the ceremony was unforgettable. I motioned to Aunt Camilla and she handed me the folded piece of paper. I read the writing on the paper carefully and deliberately to make sure that he could hear every word I said and the meaning behind them.

"Aaron, the first thing that I must do is thank God and then thank you for listening to God. We would not be here if it were not for your discernment and relationship with Him. You have been the man that I never even knew I needed. Your light, knowledge, insight, and wisdom has lit up my world. Who you are has helped me understand the character of God, how a man should love a woman, and that love has no boundaries when it is done by way of the limitless God Almighty.

You pushed me to step out of my comfort zone, you picked me up when I was at the lowest, I had ever been in my life, and even though you took a break from me, you never abandoned me. You have respected me, treated me like a queen and a masterpiece, and helped restore a piece of me that I thought had died a while ago. You are my best

198

friend, my man, and my husband in a few minutes. I submit to you, Aaron, because you have completely and selflessly submitted yourself to God."

I looked back up at him and he was wiping his eyes with a cloth that his friend had handed him earlier. After he gathered himself, he reached into his pocket to pull out his piece of folded paper, and then he started to read.

"Mya, I always thought I was fully aware of who I was, but when I met you, you revealed to me that I was so much more. You took my patience, selflessness, love, manhood and purpose to another level. You made me work for what I knew was meant to be mine and I was okay with that. When you entered my life, I heard God speak to me many times telling me that you were going to change my life and that you were the only person for me. If I had not listened, I would have been either alone or with the wrong person. The time that it took me to get to this point with you is time that I wouldn't trade for anything in the world. Every step that we took to get here was worth it. The time that we spent separated was worth it. You are absolutely worth it and I plan on giving you the world and more. Thank you for being the woman that God called you to be first and then my woman second. I love you."

After Aaron finished his vows and I finished drying my eyes, it was time for us to complete the rest of the ceremony and be officially married. We walked over to a side table where there were two slender, glass containers of sand, one gold and one pink. He picked up the gold and I picked up the pink and we began to pour these together at once to ensure that the sand would mix. This signified that we could never be separated, that all of our thoughts, dreams, wishes, and every small and big thing in our life was now blended. Then, on that same table, we signed our papers that represented the legality of our marriage. After that, we walked back to the altar, repeated a few things after Pastor Gerard, and as soon as we heard, "I now present to you Mr. and Mrs. Aaron Journey," we kissed and began our descent back down the aisle.

As we danced down the aisle, I spotted Mike, Dr. Horia, Mrs. Lamire, Noelle's family, and a few other distant family members and friends on both his side of the family and mine. We danced, smiled, and waved as we exited the doors of the building. The videographer had filmed everything, and the photographer had taken all of the pictures that he possibly could. At the end, we were asked to take pictures with everyone which would be a great future memory for us to look back at every year we grew together.

We chose to have a small gathering at my parent's house for the reception. When we got there, the people that my parents hired had decorated the place in pink and gold, there was a beautiful cake that looked like it shouldn't even be eaten, and there was the smell of delicious food that the caterers had prepared. As people came in, they would lay their gifts on a table and then grab a glass of champagne. When most of the guests had arrived, my mother and father requested everyone's attention and my mother began to speak.

"Even though getting to this day has not been easy, this has not only been a miraculous day, but it has been a miraculous journey of years full of ups and downs. We are so blessed to see our daughter so happy and healthy and we are equally blessed to see the man that God has placed in her life.

"Aaron, thank you for all you have done and for who you are. You are absolutely perfect for our daughter and we love you. Mya, thank you for who you are. Your transformation has been something rare. We couldn't ask for more from you because you have made us such proud parents."

Her voice got shaky and a tear dropped from her eye. "I also want to address Noelle's parents and tell you thank you for being here. We all love you so much." She nodded towards them and smiled.

My father then stepped up and said, "A toast to a beautiful, fulfilling, and everlasting marriage for two extraordinary people, Mya and Aaron. We love you." Everyone lifted up their glasses in a toast before taking a sip.

The rest of the reception was laid back. The food was beyond amazing and the conversations and advice was heart-warming. After everyone had eaten, it wasn't much longer before they were telling us goodbye as they made their way to the front door and we were cleaning up.

The four of us, my mom, dad, Aaron, and I, sat on the couch for a while as we took in the day. We finally had a sense of time since it had moved extremely fast all day.

After a little while of silence, my mom turned to us and said, "So tomorrow's the day that you two officially move into your new home together, huh?"

Thinking about this made me feel like my insides were twinkling. "Yes, ma'am," Aaron said.

"How does it feel?" She asked.

"Unbelievable. New. Even though those words don't really encompass the feelings." He responded.

"What can we do?" My dad chimed in.

"There is not much else to do since most of our things are in the house already. I just have to pack up the things that I had here with me. You two have done more than enough. Thank you so much!" I got up and started making my way to the stairs.

"Wait. Before you go upstairs for the night, we got you two something for you to take back." My dad ran upstairs and then came back with a large picture of the "love is" verses from 1 Corinthians 13 in the Bible. It had pink and gold letters gracefully printed on a black background with a wooden frame. It was gorgeous.

"We thought that it would be nice to go above your wedding photos if you two decide to hang them up in your home." My mother said.

"Thank you so much! This is amazing," I said.

"Wow. You two actually love us." Aaron said which made everyone laugh. "Thank you, seriously."

I hugged them and then went upstairs to pack up as many things as I could. My mother followed me up but went to her bedroom and Aaron decided to stay downstairs and speak with my dad. I took a shower, wrote about this extraordinary day in my journal, and went to bed. Even though today exceeded anything that I could have ever imagined, I was drained. I didn't even feel Aaron crawl into bed next to me.

The next morning, we woke up and immediately became busy with packing up the rest of my things, loading them in the car, making sure my parent's home was cleaned, and then preparing for the two-hour ride to our humble abode. After everything was in place for us to leave, we all sat at the table for breakfast, and then we said our goodbyes.

As soon as we sat in the car, we prayed for safe travels and we thanked God for everything that had transpired. There was a presence that we both recognized as the Spirit of God and we prayed that it would not only stay in our car as we travelled, but that it would invade our entire life, our home, our workplaces, and more.

Because it was so early when we made it home, we decided that we would go on a date to kick off our staycation. We first took the time to take all of my things out of the car and place them in the vicinity of where they would go in our home. I was so glad that Aaron and my parents had already moved most of the things in.

After we had gotten cleaned up and dressed for our date we were back in the car and headed to a spot that Aaron found online. The place had a relaxing atmosphere with soft music playing in the background. We were seated as soon as we arrived, and they brought us water and different types of bread to start us off.

A little while later, we had ordered our food and were eating as we talked about all of the events that had taken place so quickly within the last month. We finally had time to ourselves to laugh, talk, flirt, and be completely alone. As we were sitting at that table, I prayed that the rest of our marriage would be full of times like these; simple but beautiful times like these.

When we got home, we showered and watched a movie before we both drifted off to sleep. The last thing that I thought about before I slipped into sleep was that this past month had moved so fast, yet, it had been unimaginable and beyond my wildest dreams. God had showed out and it almost felt unreal.

Part 3: The Awakening

Chapter 19

"Honey! Wake up! She's waking up! She's moving!" My dad was practically yelling.

Why is he so loud? I heard shuffling from my right side and then I felt another person standing near me. I opened my eyes to bright lights and, when my eyes adjusted, I could see my parents standing over me with huge smiles on their face. My mother immediately grabbed me into a huge hug while my father was almost jumping off of his feet with excitement. *What is going on? Why are they so excited?*

"What's going on?" My voice sounded so groggy as if I was in the deepest sleep of my life. I tried to sit up, but my father was quick to tell me to relax before my mother ran to the door to grab the closest nurse.

I kept hearing my mother say, "She's awake!" I had just laid down to take a nap, but I was not where I laid down initially. I was in ... a hospital. I was trying to think of every scenario that could have happened that brought me back to yet another hospital. Did I fall? Did I break a bone? Was I in a car wreck?

I felt myself say "stop," but it was not loud enough because the quick-paced shuffling continued. I then felt myself yell "stop" and everyone looked at me and came to my side. "What is going on? Why am I back in the hospital?"

"Back? Honey, you never left the hospital. You have been here for about two weeks. Do you remember the fire?"

"The fire? Of course, I remember the fire. I lost my best friend. Where is that water? How long have I been asleep? I am so hungry and thirsty."

My father reached for the glass of water sitting on the tray near the bed, handed it to me and said, "You were found on the ground outside of the home the night of the fire. You were brought here, and you have remained asleep the entire time. The doctors couldn't find anything wrong with you that would cause a coma."

"What? No Aaron? No Grace? No Goshen Psychiatric Hospital? What about Dr. Horia? I didn't complete school?"

"Honey, what are you talking about? No. We don't know those people. I'm sorry. I know this is a very confusing time, but we need you to relax so that the doctors can make sure that you're okay." My mother said.

I allowed my body to lay back on the hospital bed because I thought about all that I had just experienced and how it was all apparently just a dream. I almost felt a feeling of deep despair settle in because none of it was true. I didn't meet Aaron and get married. I didn't even know if such an amazing man existed.

After sulking for a while, I felt the comforting presence of God come over me and remind me that He allowed me to experience an alternate reality because He needed me to establish a relationship with Him for myself,

208

He wanted me to be still and listen, He needed me to learn His character and who He was now and who He had always been even back when the Israelites were in the wilderness. He reminded me that my life would be exceedingly and abundantly more than I could ever imagine, and that the lessons that I learned in the dream that He provided me would be necessary in my journey through the real world.

Within the next few minutes, a large group of people had crowded into my small hospital room. I was so caught up in my thoughts that I wasn't even paying attention to the person who was checking my vital signs, but when I looked up, it was Dr. Horia. I tried not to leap out of my bed and hug her because I wasn't sure if I had met her in real life or in the dream.

"Hi, Mya, I am Dr. Horia. It's nice to finally meet you. How are you feeling?"

Well, that confirmed that we had never met. I tried not to sigh out loud, but I was a little disappointed. "I feel okay," I mumbled.

"Mya, we have definitely been keeping an eye on you. You gave us a scare because we just couldn't seem to understand or locate the cause for your coma. It was almost like you were just in a deep sleep. We're elated that you're now awake and alert."

"Thanks," I said. I needed time to actually process what was going on. I felt the urge to write everything down thanks to my dream Dr. Horia. I put a journal on my mental list for when I was released from here.

209

After Dr. Horia got done examining me and drawing some blood, she said, "Well, Mya, I would like to run these blood samples to the lab and, after we get results back and depending on what the results reveal, we will determine when you will be able to leave." I simply nodded and told her thank you again.

Soon after she left the room, my mother told me that she had contacted one of the associate pastors and the Christian counselor from their church. She let him know that I was awake and that she would like for him to come and pray over us and the lab results.

About an hour later, the associate pastor came walking through the door and, I should have guessed, it was none other than Mike. "Hi, Mya. I have heard so much about you and have been up here to visit with you and your family quite a few times along with my brother. How are you feeling?"

"Just another alternate universe connection." I thought to myself and instantly felt guilty for my slight attitude. "I'm well. Thanks for asking."

"While you were asleep, I thought about some things and I would like to talk to you about that. Would you be okay with just the two of us talking?"

"Absolutely." I said quickly. I just knew that he was about to say something that I needed to hear.

After everyone left, he handed me a journal and a matching pen that was in his hand. "This is for you. My brother, who is also in ministry, and I decided that this would be a great gift for when you woke up to help you make sense of all of your thoughts. I wasn't sure at first, but he was adamant as if he knew you personally."

I shook my head and said, "thank you." This was a lot for me to grasp and I had just made a mental note to purchase a journal to make my thoughts plain. Coming from Mike, this was no coincidence.

"So, Mya, I know that this is overwhelming for you, but I sense something different about your situation. Earlier, I stated that you were asleep rather than using the term "coma" because your parents explained to me that the medical professionals couldn't find any internal or external injuries that could explain your unconscious state. With that being said, I wanted to ask you if you were aware of what was going on around you while you were in that state for the last two weeks?"

I thought for a second and then I said, "No, I wasn't aware of my surroundings. Maybe I wouldn't have been so confused when I woke up to my parents yelling over me." I chuckled a little.

"Right. After thinking and praying about it, the only thing that I could come up with was that this was a spiritual event for you. Do you agree?"

This was the exact same Mike from my dream. I looked at him for a minute in astonishment because that's exactly what had taken place within me. Not only did I go through an alternate life where I learned about God, but He was gracious enough to bring me out of my sleeping state and into my actual life where he was beginning to reveal something even more grand to me.

211

"I agree 100 percent," I replied.

I then took the time to tell him the whole entire alternate life dream experience. I talked for almost two hours and he sat there and listened to everything from the Dissociative Identity Disorder to Goshen Psychiatric Hospital to me meeting him, Aaron, and Dr. Horia. Every part of my story was coming out like word vomit. When I finally finished, I took a deep breath because apparently, I didn't breathe the entire time.

Mike sat silent for a few beats while shaking his head and looking at me as if he wanted to say, "I knew it!" He then said, "I believe everything you said because I sensed that your state was deeper than just a coma. You know, I absolutely love how God took the terms 'rest' and 'be still' to a different level. He needed you to receive something big and, according to everything you just told me, you will be able to reach the masses in ways that you never thought you would. I also find it kind of nice that God allowed you to heal basically in your sleep from the death of Noelle." He shook his head as if he was amazed by what God had done.

"I think that's how I look at it as well. I know my healing process would have been completely different had I been coherent to experience everything. Also, I honestly can't wait to see what God has in store and what He plans on doing with such a unique experience."

"Right! And also, I have someone that I need you to meet when you are able to come to your parent's church." He had a huge smile on his face.

"Who is it that you would like me to meet?"

"My brother. Even though he came here with me multiple times to visit you, he would be excited to officially meet you. There was an odd connection with you two where you would move and even smile when he was around. Very odd." He gazed into space with a face of satisfaction as if he knew something that I didn't know.

"Interesting, well, I am absolutely ready to get out of here and interact with everyone in passing. I feel like I have missed so much. I don't feel like there is anything wrong with me."

"Well, we will be here for when you get out and long after. I have really enjoyed hearing about your alternate life and your perspective. I hope that you will be willing to talk to me more after you transition out of here." He stood up to leave.

"Thank you so much for coming and being able to understand what I was talking about. We will definitely continue our talk once I'm out." I smiled and he shook my hand as if I were fragile.

When he left the room, my mother, father, and Aunt Camilla came rushing back in. My aunt rushed over to me and gave me a bear hug before she even said hello. I was just as happy to see her, though.

"How do you feel? I have missed you so much!" She hugged me again.

"I feel perfectly fine and hungry." I laughed. "I missed you, too!" We hugged a third time. My parents scooted some chairs near the bed and we all just started to talk and get caught up. Even though it was only two weeks, it seemed like forever and it seemed to me like I had missed so much. I was also a little sad because we talked about Noelle, her funeral, and how I had to miss it due to my state. I felt a glimmer of guilt, but I remembered those things that Dr. Horia told me in my alternate reality.

We ate, talked for a couple of hours, and laughed until it was time for Aunt Camilla to leave and for us all to get some rest. My father went home, and my mother crawled up on the couch beside me for the night. When she fell asleep, I chose to write a brief entry in my new journal to represent the beginning of my new life.

"This whole situation could have been completely different. I could have reacted differently, thought differently, perceived differently, but I didn't. God, what you instilled in me, what you taught me is something that cannot be taken away, dulled by my comeback to reality, or even crushed by the realization that all that I had going on there, is not here. The transformation and the newness of my intangible characteristics allows me to fully accept and be grateful for my sleeping state. I would not trade my circumstances for the world because I experienced God firsthand, I healed, I loved, I grew. I also know that he blessed me tremendously in a world that didn't even exist so I know that my blessings here will be even more. I expect so much from God because He has shown me so much. If only everyone could receive the fullness of God. It is an incomprehensible and inexplicable feeling. I am fulfilled, I am now, and I am ready."

I shut my journal and placed it on the stand next to the bed. I drifted into a sleep where I didn't experience anything except pure peace.

I was awakened at about six o' clock in the morning to chattering. When I opened my eyes, my mother said, "Good news, Mya!! We're being discharged today."

Before I could speak, Dr. Horia chimed in and said, "Mya, your situation is perplexing because your lab results and vitals all came back almost perfect. There didn't even seem to be anything pointing to the fact that you weren't eating as much as a normal person would or your lessened intake of water during your coma. It is highly bizarre, but there is nothing left for us to do but send you home. We would like for you to come back once a week for a month to make sure that nothing arises."

"I don't believe that you will find anything. I feel better than I ever have, but I am more than willing to come back to make sure that everything remains positive."

"Thank you." Dr. Horia stated as she clasped her hands together. "We will start preparing you for discharge, disconnect everything from you, and get your discharge paperwork situated and then you all can get out of here." She waited for us to acknowledge what she said and then she turned and walked out of the door.

My parents started straightening everything while the nurse started removing needles and tubes from me. A little while later, we had received the discharge paperwork and were headed out of the front door of the hospital.

About an hour later, we made it to my parent's home where we were greeted by Frenzie, the cat, who rubbed her body along both of my ankles, Aunt Camillla, and the amazing smell of a home cooked meal. Just as excited as she was when I first woke up, my aunt ran up to me and hugged me tightly. She was such a light. I hugged her back just as tightly. She stepped back, looked at me, and said, "You look hungry! Are you hungry?" She laughed and turned towards the kitchen.

"Yes, but even if I weren't, I would still eat this meal. It smells so good!" I said this as I started walking towards my room to put my things down.

Soon after, we were all sitting at the dinner table eating a meal while we discussed if I would be up to going to church tomorrow. I let them know that I would be happy to go and that I didn't feel like there should be any delay in me merging into a normal routine, but that I would take it easy until after all of my follow-up appointments were complete. My family was comfortable with my plan as long as I didn't try to do "too much." Apparently, they didn't understand that doing too much wouldn't harm me because I was divinely healed and prepared to restart my life.

After dinner, we all went to our rooms and Aunt Camilla went home. I took a shower and chose my clothes for the next day - a beautiful floral dress and some heels to go with it. I wasn't sure why I felt a surge of excitement when I thought about meeting Mike's brother. I guess I wanted to understand why we had a connection even

216

though we didn't know one another. I was so ready to sleep in a comfortable bed that didn't belong to the hospital, so I turned on the television and watched it from bed until I drifted off into slumber.

The next morning, I was awakened by the smell of breakfast and the purring of Frenzie who had apparently snuck into my room and bed some time during the night. I stroked her soft fur a few times and then got up and walked downstairs. "Good morning!" my mother said as she drifted over to me. "Do you want coffee? Tea? You hungry?"

"Mom, you don't have to do all of this. I can fix myself some coffee and a plate. Thank you for cooking." I chuckled. I needed to remind her that I was fully capable of operating in the kitchen.

"Okay. Well, help yourself. We need to be leaving by 10:30. We need to get a good parking spot and get in the building before 11:00." I glanced at the clock. It was now 9:35 so I needed to hurry up and eat and get dressed.

It took me maybe 15 minutes to eat and drink my coffee and then I went upstairs to dress myself. It took me a minute to find my curling iron and makeup which was stowed away underneath the bathroom cabinet in a mess of other things. I curled my hair, did my makeup, and put on the dress which was just a little too big for me since I had lost some weight while being in the hospital. Either way, I looked beautiful. I slipped on my heels and walked down the stairs to meet my parents.

217

Twenty minutes later, we were parking the car and stepping into the church. There had been so many changes to this church since Noelle and I went off to college, so I was looking forward to seeing them. Also, the church was huge which explained why I had never met Mike, his brother, or many other people, I was sure.

At the entrance to the sanctuary, we were greeted by a woman who gave us a program and directed us to a seat. As soon as we found our seat, we were right back on our feet for praise and worship which seemed to be more modernized with a concert vibe. As I was clapping my hands, I was looking around to see if I recognized anyone and I spotted Mike on the front row to the left. The smile on his face when he told me that he wanted me to meet someone had given me even more motivation to come today.

After praise and worship, someone came up on the stage and made a few announcements and then the lead pastor, whom I remember, came up on the stage and jumped right into the message which was called "Cloud 9" which was a part of his "Contentment" series. I was so grateful that I had brought my journal and my Bible.

Throughout the message, I realized that it seemed as if the pastor was speaking directly to me, so I made sure to write down the points that really touched me.

- *1 Timothy 6:6-7 Now godliness with contentment is great gain. For we brought nothing into this world, and it is certain that we can carry nothing out.*

218

- *Colossians 3:1-2 If then you were raised with Christ, seek those things which are above, where Christ is, sitting at the right hand of God. Set your mind on things above, not on things on the earth.*
- *Thinking on a higher level allows us to be content in knowing that we will not be able to see past what is right in front of us, but that we know that there is greater in store. We cannot allow what is in front of us to keep us from seeking the higher things.*
- *When we think about Cloud 9, we think about how nothing can make our happiness waver in that moment. We think about how we are floating due to the positive results of a certain situation. We can always be on cloud 9 when we fix our mind on those things that are above.*
- *What are those higher things that you should be seeking in your life?*
- *Fix your gaze upward. Why focus on those things that we ultimately have no control over?*
- *What temporary things are holding our gaze and keeping us from looking higher?*
- *God doesn't want us literally looking up and oblivious to the world. He wants our perspectives to align with His Word. Our motivations, actions, reactions, words, and focus will determine our alignment.*

This message was more like a confirmation to me to let me know that my perspective was in the right place.

219

After church had ended, I turned around to place my Bible and journal back into my bag and, when I turned back around, my mother and father were talking to Mike. When he saw me look at him, he said, "Hey, Mya! How are you?"

"I'm good. You?"

"Good. Good. I want you to meet my brother. He stepped to the side and tapped on the shoulder of the man that was standing directly behind him speaking with someone else with his back turned to us. The man responded to the tap by turning around.

I should have known that God would show out in the most unexpected ways. I trusted Him and He continued to give me reasons as to why I should.

"Hi," he said as he turned. And then he saw me and said, "Hey!" even louder and rushed up to hug me. The hug felt so natural like we had known each other forever. He hugged me like we had had a million conversations previously. He stepped back again and said, "Mya! It's so great to finally meet you. I guess I could have told you my name before I rushed you. I'm Aaron."

I knew his name as soon as I saw that beautiful face. "I'm Mya. It's so great to meet you as well. Your brother told me that you were coming in and checking on me while I was in the hospital. I would like to thank you so much for that."

"Of course. I would love for us to go out for lunch one day and talk about your experience. Mike didn't tell me much, but he did tell me that you had a remarkable and unforgettable time during your sleep."

By this time, my parents had gone off to talk with other people who were also still lingering in the church. "I would love that as well. You can take my number down and then text or call when you would like to meet." I gave him my number when he pulled out his phone. We talked a little bit longer, hugged once more, and then went our separate ways for the time being.

Chapter 20

Two Years Later

God told me that my life would be abundantly and exceedingly more than I could ever imagine when I woke up in the hospital from my alternate reality dream. I trusted Him and now I was married to Aaron, we lived in a home similar to the one from my dream, and I was the Director of Human Resources of a resource center for mental health illnesses that our church opened up in Richmond, Virginia. Aaron is the Corporate Operations Officer of the same organization.

According to the test results and follow up appointments with Dr. Horia, I am one of the healthiest people she had ever seen. And, to top it all off, Aaron and I had a puppy named Grace that was Aaron's before he'd ever met me or knew my story.

Aaron and I began courting one another almost immediately after I met him that Sunday after church. We went on a date and were pretty much inseparable after that. We built our relationship on God's foundation and with transparency, honesty, and fun. About six months into us dating, Aaron and I went to Honolulu, Hawaii for a getaway since it had been so long since either one of us had been on a vacation. There, he proposed to me at sunset during the beach picnic that he had planned. He was just as amazing or maybe even more amazing than he had been in my dream. He was better than the man of my dreams.

Throughout the time before our wedding, we were in the process of looking for a home together. I was still living with my parents and he was living in an apartment. We were not exactly sure where we were being led to live and we were not even sure if we were supposed to stay in the same city. Despite the difficulties, we just knew that everything would work out perfectly.

Six months later, Aaron and I went to the courthouse with a
few friends and family members and had a quick ceremony. The ceremony was beautiful and, afterwards, we went to my parent's house to celebrate, eat, and fellowship. We were both extremely joyful as this was something that we had both prayed for. We were in this for life.

Also, about six months after everything was back to what we would consider normal, I had gotten heavily involved in the church and was eventually added to the staff as a part-time employee. During this time, my relationship with Mike and the lead pastors had grown tremendously. They trusted me to get work done, noticed my outstanding work ethic, and appreciated the professional relationships that I had built with other employees. Eventually, they asked how I would feel about working in the Human Resource realm. I told them that I would love it as long as I had the proper training. They began training me to make sure that I was prepared for what they were going to ask next.

Simultaneously, Aaron was being groomed to work in operations. His training seemed to be a little more extensive than mine, but we both loved that they were bettering and educating us even though we had no clue what was to come.

The lead pastor, Pastor Omar, scheduled a meeting with me randomly about two weeks before Aaron and I were set to get married. He also asked Aaron to meet with him an hour after my meeting was set. We were a little confused and nervous about what was going on, but we were optimistic.

"Hi, Mya. How are you doing?" Pastor Omar asked.

"I'm great, Pastor. How are you?"

"That's good to hear. I'm well. I'm sure you're wondering why I asked you to meet with me today?" He looked down as he gathered some papers and then looked back at me. I nodded. "I would first like to state that this is something that has not yet been announced to the church or other staff members just yet, so we would like for you to keep everything confidential for the time being. Okay?"

"Yes, sir." I agreed.

"We are in the final stages of opening up a mental health resource center in Richmond, Virginia. This will be an area for people in the mental health field to get training and train others which is where our prospective Director of Education will come in. People will be able to receive mental health outpatient services, there will be a yoga studio, a meditation room, a small seminar room, smaller rooms for counseling sessions, and a chapel.

"With that being said, we have been observing you through your everyday work for the last couple of months and through the recent training and we believe that you would be an extraordinary Director of Human Resources that would represent the company well. We do have others that we are looking to hire for other positions like a licensed professional counselor, a psychiatrist, and some support staff, but we have only been looking at you for this particular position. Before you say anything," he continued, "I would like to let you know that this center is being advertised and we already have a waiting list of clients so it will be very fast paced. What do you think?"

"Wow. This was totally unexpected, but it sounds amazing. It sounds like this is the opportunity of a lifetime and I believe that I am ready to take this on. Thank you so much for considering me and I would love to take you up on that offer."

"This is great, Mya! From this point forward, we will be getting you all of the necessary paperwork and more training that you will need before you two move. We have a little while, but we want to make sure that you are all set."

"This is great. I am looking forward to the process and the transition. I look forward to hearing from you more about the details."

"You will probably get tired of hearing from me about this, but I believe it will be worth it. You can start

225

by reading over this job description and information on the center before our next meeting which will be next week if that works for you." He gathered up the papers on his desk and handed them to me.

"Thank you." I took the papers from him. "Next week works perfectly fine. Thank you so much, Pastor." I reached out my hand to shake his and I left the room. I thought to myself, "Even though I truly wanted to finish school and get my degree, this transition into the director of Human Resource was God's way of reminding me that degrees are not way-makers, He is."

When Aaron saw me, I gave no indication of what was going on because I wanted him to be as surprised and happy as I was when he heard the good news. I had no clue what job they would offer him, but I knew that it had to do with operations since his training was in that field. Thirty minutes later, when Aaron came out of the office, he was smiling from ear to ear and I knew that he had some good news to share just as I did.

We walked to the car in silence and, when we got in, we looked at one another and started clapping and laughing and celebrating what had just happened. We even said a quick prayer to thank God for what He was doing in our lives.

"So, tell me, what position were you offered, Mya?"

"I've accepted the position of the Director of Human Resources!"

"That's major! Sounds like a boss to me."

"And what position were you offered?"

"I gladly and ever so gratefully accepted the position of ..." He did a drum roll on the steering wheel. "Corporate Operations Officer! Mr. COO!"

"Aaron! That's awesome! I am so proud of you. All of your hard work has paid off."

"I am proud of us. I know that this road will not always be this easy, but it will all be worth it as long as we continue operating with God in the middle of everything."

"Agreed." I smiled and grabbed his hand.

"It sounds like Richmond is the move. I knew there was a reason as to why we couldn't find the perfect place here." Aaron said.

The home that we found was perfect and even better than the one in the alternate life. After settling into our new home and marriage, Aaron and I were getting into the swing of things at our jobs. In that time, we found a gym, a yoga studio, and some things that we could do to keep us from getting bored. I chose not to use the yoga studio at my place of employment because I wanted to utilize a sauna, which was at the yoga studio I chose, and I wanted to meet more people outside of work. I established a schedule of yoga every evening to keep me healthy. I had even met a group of women at yoga who invited me to brunch with them. Aaron decided to invest in a gym membership where he eventually met some people that could potentially be good friends as well.

When work began, we continued to maintain our afternoon schedules of the gym and yoga. On the weekends, we went on dates and would even have date and movie nights at home.

I had pretty much gotten used to who would be at yoga in the last two weeks. I had established my place in the yoga studio and had formed connections with the other women working and attending sessions there. One day, a woman that I didn't recognize was at the studio. Unfortunately, I didn't have time to introduce myself before class started. And by the end of the session, I was tired from a busy day at work, so I said my goodbyes quickly before leaving.

I made it home shortly where Aaron and I ate dinner while we talked about our day. Afterward, I told him that I was going to go to bed, and he stayed in the living room watching television. This ended up being the first night that I had one of the weird dreams similar to the ones in my alternate reality. When I woke up, I took out my journal and began to write about it.

"The dream basically showed my life how it was currently. I was married to Aaron, I lived in the same home, I worked at the same job, I went to the same yoga classes, and we drove the same car. The only difference was that I felt like someone was always watching. I would be walking from my home to the car and then I would immediately stop because I sensed something behind me. I would be walking from the car to the yoga studio and I would quickly turn to glance behind me to see if anyone was watching me. After a while experiencing this and not telling anyone what was going on, I took matters into my

228

own hands. I watched everyone and everything around me which drove me crazy. One night, as I was leaving my yoga class, I had that same eerie feeling and when I turned around, I was standing there facing myself who was dressed in tattered and dirty clothing with messy hair and a sad and droopy face.

Interpretation: The yoga studio showed up twice in this dream. There was a difference in the yoga studio yesterday. It was the person that I had not paid much attention to. Was this dream triggered due to the presence of this new person? Also, that constant feeling of being watched could be interpreted also as afraid, nervous, anxious, and more. The fact that I was the one who was watching myself is interesting. I believe that it could represent the fact that I could possibly be my own enemy or that I have nothing to be afraid of because I am the only person that exists within me, right?

I quickly shut my journal before my mind went off on a tangent. I couldn't allow myself to think too deeply about what that dream could have meant. I did make a mental note to introduce myself to the newcomer the next time I saw her though. I got my opportunity to do just that the next night.

When she first walked into class, I caught a glimpse of her, and she looked vaguely familiar. I brushed it off because I knew that I had never met her before. I finished the class and, before she could approach the door to leave, I approached her and introduced myself. Before

229

she could respond, I grew lightheaded because I recognized her as soon as she faced me directly.

I woke up, once again, in a hospital. My voice was groggy when I asked, "Why am I here again?"

"I received a call from your yoga studio. They found my information on your emergency contact form." Aaron responded as he took my hand.

Slowly, everything began to come back to me. I reminded Aaron of my alternate identity in my alternate reality and how many people from there were showing up here. I then told him that when I went to introduce myself to the new woman in my yoga class it was Meira dressed in yoga clothing.

We sat quietly, him in the chair and me in the hospital bed, and I reminded myself of something that I read and wrote in my journal in my alternate life. It stated "It's not about what ailments you have, whether they are physical or mental. It's about how you handle what you have." In this case, it's not about what comes up against me, it's about how I react and the weapons that I choose to use.

Epilogue

God prepared me to deal with this a long time ago when I was in my alternate life. He knew that I would be able to handle it because He properly equipped me. He helped me form a totally new perspective, He taught me how to use spiritual weapons, and He showed me the importance of being transparent with a supportive community. I got this.

In the alternate reality, I had to be admitted to the mental health hospital due to an attempted suicide. This time, I will go through the process of outpatient so whatever is going on mentally won't manifest itself into my life physically. So that it won't take control over me.

I will not ruin the beautiful life that God has given me because I am afraid. I will get counseling, I will tell my loving husband what is going on, I will be open to my family and friends, I will spread my testimony, and I will celebrate in times of trial and tribulation.

No more pain, no more fear, no more losses, and no more stigma.

-- Mya Afad-Journey

Discussion Questions

1. Why do you believe that conversations around mental health are still considered a stigma?
2. In what ways do you believe that the stigma of mental health and the stigmata or crucifixion wounds of Christ come together in this book?
3. Trauma impacts each and every one of us in different ways. In what ways were you able to relate to the way that Mya's trauma impacted her? What unique ways did trauma impact you and how did you handle it?
4. What does healing mean to you and in what ways have you been healed?
5. Describe your relationship with God using three words. What can you do to enhance those words or the relationship?
6. Because we are human beings, it is easy for us to place God in our realm which causes Him to be limited, but in what ways has God shown you or reminded you that He is limitless?
7. What is your purpose and how is it meant to impact the lives of other people?
8. Utilizing your support system is important. What would you share about others about getting and maintaining a support system? If they don't have one, how would you go about explaining how to obtain one?
9. What physical or mental characteristics do you have that you would consider an ailment? How do you believe that God can use that for His glorification?

Names and Terms:

Ahlai Foe (Ah-Lay-ee Fo): Sorrowing experience

Meira (Mih-Ra): one who gives light; illuminate

Stigma: Refers to something shameful that is attached to a person, concept, or subject; known to cause disgrace.

Stigmata (Stig-Ma-Ta): Latin plural form of stigma. Crucifixion wounds of Jesus Christ

234